DEMI

THE ITALIAN CARTEL #6

SHANDI BOYES

COPYRIGHT

Written By: Shandi Boyes

Cover: SSB Covers & Design

Editing: Nikki @ Swish Design & Editing

Proofreading: Kaylene @ Swish Design & Editing.

Photography: Stock Photo

WANT TO STAY IN TOUCH?

Facebook: facebook.com/authorshandi

Instagram: instagram.com/authorshandi

Email: authorshandi@gmail.com

Reader's Group: bit.ly/ShandiBookBabes

Website: authorshandi.com

Newsletter: subscribepage.com/AuthorShandi

DEDICATION

To those going through difficult times,
The sun always shines no matter how dark the clouds, and so do you.

Shandi xx

ALSO BY SHANDI BOYES

Denotes Standalone Books

<u>Perception Series</u>

<u>Saving Noah</u> *

<u>Fighting Jacob</u> *

<u>Taming Nick</u> *

<u>Redeeming Slater</u> *

<u>Saving Emily</u>

<u>Wrapped Up with Rise Up</u>

<u>Protecting Nicole</u> *

<u>Enigma</u>

<u>Enigma</u>

<u>Unraveling an Enigma</u>

<u>Enigma The Mystery Unmasked</u>

<u>Enigma: The Final Chapter</u>

<u>Beneath The Secrets</u>

<u>Beneath The Sheets</u>

<u>Spy Thy Neighbor</u> *

<u>The Opposite Effect</u> *

<u>I Married a Mob Boss</u> *

Second Shot *

The Way We Are

The Way We Were

Sugar and Spice *

Lady In Waiting

Man in Queue

Couple on Hold

Enigma: The Wedding

Silent Vigilante

Hushed Guardian

Quiet Protector

Enigma: An Isaac Retelling

Twisted Lies *

Bound Series

Chains

Links

Bound

Restrain

The Misfits *

Nanny Dispute *

Russian Mob Chronicles

Nikolai: A Mafia Prince Romance

Nikolai: Taking Back What's Mine

Nikolai: What's Left of Me

Nikolai: Mine to Protect

Asher: My Russian Revenge *

Nikolai: Through the Devil's Eyes

Trey *

The Italian Cartel

Dimitri

Roxanne

Reign

Mafia Ties (Novella)

Maddox

Demi

Ox

Rocco *

Clover *

Smith *

RomCom Standalones

Just Playin' *

Ain't Happenin' *

The Drop Zone *

Very Unlikely *

False Start *

<u>**Short Stories - Newsletter Downloads**</u>

Christmas Trio *

Falling For A Stranger *

<u>**One Night Only Series**</u>

Hotshot Boss *

Hotshot Neighbor *

<u>**The Bobrov Bratva Series**</u>

Wicked Intentions *

Sinful Intentions *

Devious Intentions *

Deadly Intentions *

1

MADDOX

"Maddox…"

When Demi reaches out for me, I suck in a relieved breath. It does little to loosen the knot in my stomach, but the benefits to my screaming lungs are incomparable. I thought she was dead, or at the very worst, on her way to death. This is the first time in my life I'm grateful for jumping the gun. She's bleeding more than she should be, is incoherent and woozy, but the blood pumping out of her isn't coming from slashes in her wrists or mortal body wounds. It's gushing from an area I'm reasonably sure she shouldn't be bleeding from, considering all three tests on the vanity sink show two bright blue lines. If the amount of red liquid pooling in the bottom of the shower is anything to go by, I'm also certain it's more than Demi's life that's on the line right now.

"I'm s-s-so cold," she mutters through chattering teeth.

"I know, baby. I'll get you warm as soon as I can. I just need to get you cleaned up a bit first…" My words trail off when the shiver wreaking havoc with Demi's tiny frame doubles in strength. She's shuddering like she is in an ice bath, and her lips are turning blue.

"Demi…"

I slap her cheek in an endeavor to rouse her. The image of my hand tapping the scar on her right cheek kills me, but I'd rather her face be reddened by my hand than whitened by death.

"Stay with me, baby. Come on, just a little longer. The medics are on their way."

When she fails to respond to my begs for her to hold on, I snag her dressing gown off the back of the bathroom door, carefully place it around her shoulders, then scoop her into my arms. My race out of the cabin is so desperate, my body fails to register the coolness of the crisp lawn on my bare feet, much less the fact I only have my motorbike at my disposal. Demi only whimpered when I thrust her into my chest. There's no way she'll make the twenty-mile trip to the hospital on the back of my bike.

I stop seeking the sounds of a siren on the horizon when the crunch of dead leaves under a boot sounds through my ears. Weeks ago, I would have said it was the armed goons Dimitri placed on each entrance of the property, but when my first couple of fights occurred without a single sneer from Col, the number of men guarding the cabin soon dwindled to none.

I thought it was for the best. Now, I'm not so sure. I hate leaving Demi's protection in the hands of anyone not related to me by blood, but if I hadn't been so stubborn, perhaps I would have had better means to seek medical help than two wheels between a chunk of metal anarchy.

My mood doesn't know which way to swing when a big balding Russian steps out from the shadows. Unlike earlier when he witnessed the tussle between Dimitri and me, Agent Brahn isn't aiming his gun at the crinkle between my brows. His empty hands are high in the air, exposing that the gun on his hip is still fastened in its holster.

After drifting his eyes between my wet ones, Demi's white face, and the bottom of her dressing gown that's no longer stark white, he gestures for me to follow him. "You've got thirty minutes tops before she bleeds out."

My legs move before my brain can fire a single objection. I would sign on to be the devil's righthand man this very instant if he guaranteed Demi would make it out of this alive. I wasn't being facetious when I said I'd do anything to keep her safe. I killed a man, so selling my soul seems like the next logical step.

I realize how small the world's axis is when Agent Brahn breaking through the dense bushland surrounding the cabin occurs at the same time a cab pulls up in front of him. I thought he was guiding us to his government-issued vehicle. I had no clue he plans to bundle us into the back of a cab to continue our journey alone.

Too panicked to allow shock its chance to shine, I slide Demi and me through the back-passenger door Agent Brahn is holding open for me, then raise my eyes to the pair peering at me in the rearview mirror. I scarcely register their familiarity before requesting for him to take me to Mercer Private. It's the closest hospital with a permanent OBGYN. Although I wasn't smart enough to grab my shoes, I did snag the gym bag full of cash I'm rarely without these days. It should have any man side-stepping protocol. It's rare to find a man with a moral compass these days, so I won't mention the rarity of stumbling upon one in this part of the state. It isn't Hopeton, but its dealings are just as shady.

My eyes jackknife to Agent Tobias when he warns, "If you see an ambulance, continue on course. No good guys come out this far."

The blond cab driver jerks up his chin before planting his foot on the gas pedal. It's clear he and Agent Tobias have met before, but I don't have the time nor the patience to work out how far their connection goes. Demi has returned from her second bout of unconsciousness. She's clutching my drenched shirt in a white-knuckled hold while her eyes seek mine through the heaviness of hooded lids. "M-M-Mad—"

"I'm right here." I curl my shuddering hand over Demi's barren white one. "I'm not going anywhere. I'm right where I need to be. I'll never leave your side again. I promise you that."

"I-I'm sorry," she whispers through blue, shuddering lips.

I push her hair back from her face before locking my eyes with her pained ones. "What do you have to be sorry for?"

She doesn't answer me.

She doesn't need to.

The sheer terror in her eyes is very telling. She can feel the wetness seeping into her nightgown. She knows our baby's chance of survival is barely nonexistent. That doesn't make her liable, though. This isn't even on my shoulders.

"It isn't your fault. *Nothing* happening is your fault." I wipe at a rogue tear she couldn't hold back before shifting my focus to the wailing of sirens rapidly approaching us. They should offer some sort of comfort in this twisted, fucked-up day, but for some reason, they strengthen the knot in my gut instead of relinquishing its firm hold.

"Scoot down," instructs the cab driver with a backward cap and wonky grin. He's young, probably only a year or two older than Demi and me. His youth has me suspicious of his relationship with a high-up member of the FBI. Is he working with us or against us?

When the former screams the loudest of the two, I do as requested. Once I scoot Demi and me down low in our seat, the unnamed man twists his baseball cap around, then angles his head so the shadows of the early morning sun cover his face.

The gurgle of an upset stomach rolls up my esophagus when our dash past the flashing medical van has a second dose of familiarity hitting me square in the stomach. I've seen the driver of the ambulance before. He was ringside at the fight that switched me from an everyday man to a killer. He wasn't a ticket-paying customer. He was on-call to stretcher the loser out of the ring. How do I know this? The referee didn't announce the end of the fight. The paramedic did when he checked Igor for a pulse after I snapped his neck.

Remorseful yet unrepentant hazel eyes peer at me in the rearview mirror as solemn words spill from the driver's mouth. "I told you blood money would give you nothing but grief."

Acting ignorant to my scorn, the driver returns his cap to its original position before he increases his speed. With him seemingly knowing all the backstreets of Kirkland, we make it to Mercer Private remarkably quick. He barely skids to a stop at the front of the automatic double doors of the ER when I throw open the car door and curl out.

I'm hoping our arrival will replicate a blockbuster movie but am left disappointed when our race into the ER isn't greeted by a doctor in a white coat ushering us toward the first available medical bay. We're seen by a grouchy nurse seated behind a thick pane of bulletproof glass who snarls at me while pushing an admission form through a minute slot in the glass. "There's a thirty-minute delay."

"She needs to be seen before that. She's bleeding *very* heavily. She is barely conscious."

After drinking in Demi's white face and blood-soaked dressing gown, she taps her pen onto the clipboard two times before she lowers her eyes back to the paperwork in front of her. I get they're under the gun, and that they most likely have non-urgent cases all the time, but today is *not* the day for me to see sense through the madness.

"She's fuckin' bleeding! She could die. Let us in!" My anxiousness to get Demi seen is gorily exposed when I bang my fist onto the glass separating us. It smears the spotless material with Demi's blood, making the desperation in my voice pinnacle. *"Please…"*

My beg halts before it's fully issued, hindered by a faint female voice projecting across the room. "Maddox?"

While praying like fuck my family's high distinction in this state will assist me, I spin around to face the voice. Not all my prayers are answered when my eyes land on Dr. Avery, the psychiatrist Caidyn suggested I contact to speak with Demi after she was assaulted by her uncle, but her presence is better than stumbling onto an old acquaintance stuck in line with me. Avery is a doctor. She just studies people's psyche instead of their physical capabilities.

"What's going on? Why are you here?" Although she's asking

questions, she doesn't give me the chance to speak. Just like she does in her shrink chair, she seeks answers directly from the patient. "Her pupils are dilated, and her skin is pale. How long has she been wearing her nightgown?"

"Twenty, thirty minutes?" I guess, incapable of checking the time since I'd have to loosen my grip on Demi to do so. She isn't heavy. There's just no chance in hell I'd risk dropping her for a more positive response.

Dr. Avery thumps her fist onto the bulletproof glass as aggressively as me. "This patient is hemorrhaging. Call Dr. Falgar. Ask him to come to my office *immediately*." Not waiting for the nurse to respond to her snapped command, she signals for me to follow her. "Dr. Falgar is an OBGYN. He's working today, but there are no free beds in the ER." While rolling her eyes with more sophistication than a twenty-nine-year-old should have, she waves her ID card over the security lock that will gain us access to the ER. "There rarely is in this hospital."

The sound of chaos trickles into my ears when I shadow Dr. Avery's walk through the bustling ER. The nurse's lack of sympathy is understandable when I take in bay after bay after bay of patients. Each medical bay has more security personnel than it does medical staff, and almost every patient is under the influence of some sort of narcotic. They're barely coherent.

"Jesus-fucking-Christ," I mutter under my breath when it dawns on me what is happening. Karma is kicking my ass for all the bad shit I've done the past eight weeks as does the realization that the money I earned running drugs town to town was left on the cab floor. I was so eager to get Demi seen by a medical professional, I exited the taxi without my gym bag, meaning even if she comes through this with a sound mind, I don't have the means to fully remove her from it.

Fuck.

Fuck.

Fuck!

Dr. Avery's pull at this hospital is showcased in the most brilliant way when our arrival at her office occurs simultaneously with a dark-haired man I'd guess to be in his mid-thirties. He requests for me to place Demi onto the bed Dr. Avery uses to make her patients feel 'relaxed' while he dumps a set of stethoscopes onto Dr. Avery's desk.

"What are you looking for?" I ask in confusion when he thrusts up the sleeves of Demi's dressing gown instead of pushing on her stomach as I was anticipating. "She isn't an addict," I growl out when it dawns on me what he's doing. He is checking her arms for track marks.

He *tsks* me like I'm being unreasonable before he raises his eyes to Dr. Avery. The disdain on his face shifts to remorse when she briefly shakes her head. "She isn't from around these parts."

His eyes flash back to mine. They're full of silent apologies. Although annoyed at his assumption, I let it slide when his focus shifts from unearthing Demi's last 'hit' location to her midsection.

He checks her pulse, listens to her heart, then prods the lower half of her stomach. When a low, painful grunt emits from Demi's lips, her hand instinctively creeps out in search of my body, wrongly assuming it came from me. It was the same painful groan I release amid a nightmare.

I don't see Igor being the focus of my nightmares after

today, though. Demi will be responsible for both my dreams and nightmares.

I feebly shrug when Dr. Falgar asks, "How far along is she?"

"I don't know. A couple of weeks, at most."

Dr. Falgar gives me the same frustrated look he did when he arrived before racing into the corridor. When he returns with a portable ultrasound machine, Dr. Avery pushes aside the stacks of paperwork on her desk.

Although his equipment is compact, it's powerful enough for him to announce the diagnosis of an incomplete miscarriage. "Her uterine wall is extremely thick, and her cervix is open, so I'm confident in saying retained tissue is most likely the cause of the bleeding. An emergency D&C should correct it."

"But…" I ask when I hear one hanging in the air.

He waves the ultrasound wand around Demi's midsection for a couple of minutes before he locks his eyes with mine. The silent apologies of earlier have disappeared. Now, nothing but fret is seen. "More is occurring here than retained miscarriage product." I hate that he's referring to our baby as a 'product,' but his next lot of words switches my anger to worry. "Her blood isn't coagulating as it should. It's very thin and excessive. I'll order blood to be drawn when we arrive at the OR, but I may need to do a blood transfusion before the results come in."

With my head swimming with information, I steer toward the simpler part of his reply. "You're taking her to the OR now?"

As he jerks up his chin, two orderlies enter Dr. Avery's office with a gurney like you see on all the medical television shows. "If we don't *immediately* perform a D&C, she risks bleeding out."

He requests for the orderlies to be careful before he assists them with lifting Demi onto the gurney. "A standard miscarriage is usually without complications, but for someone with a blood disorder, it can be fatal."

His words knock me for a six more than any punch I've endured. "Is there anything I can do?" I feel like a helpless idiot, but my father always said it is better to offer than to leave someone stranded.

While shadowing the orderlies race down the corridor, Dr. Falgar shakes his head. "It is out of your hands now." He pushes through the flappy doors where the operating rooms are located before he shifts on his feet to face Dr. Avery. "Call her family. Better to be safe than sorry."

2

DEMI

The noise of children laughing cracks my lips into a smile. They sound truly happy like their skulls aren't throbbing as intensely as mine. I know where I am, but I feel like I'm floating instead of walking. My steps through the living room of my childhood home don't make a sound. They're lithe and free, almost as unrestricted as I felt at Seaforth Academy.

My father didn't have the funds to send me to a fancy school. The only reason I attended boarding school was because I was safer there than I was here. This property is owned by my uncle. It's one of many on his long list of properties.

You'd think my parents would have been rolling in money since they didn't have to pay rent or a mortgage, but that was far from the truth. They may not have had any debt, however, the ones they amassed with my uncle cost more than anything. He owned their souls. Not even my father's debt was relinquished when he died.

"Daddy," I choke out with a sob when my entrance into the kitchen at the back of the derelict space occurs with an image of my father sitting behind a cracked wooden table.

I shouldn't be surprised to find him here. Our family home wasn't big enough for a formal dining room, so we always ate in the kitchen. My dad loved to cook, but since that was the one thing my mother did without fault, most of our time together as a family was spent in the kitchen of my childhood home.

My father commanded the kitchen at Petretti's. It was where my love of cooking flourished, but here, in this tiny, over-spiced space, he acted as if he couldn't tell the difference between cuts of steak. He absorbed everything my mother told him while peering at her as if she was the sun, and she soaked up his attention like it didn't occur every day.

Hesitation makes itself known with my stomach when I step around the wooden dinette squashed against the side wall of the kitchen. The happy squeals of a toddler jingling in my ears aren't coming from me, the only child in this house. They're coming from a little girl my father is bouncing on his knee.

I'm on my knees in front of my dad, tickling the fair-haired girl's tummy. I must be around three or four. My knee is missing the graze it got when I assured my father I could ride my bike without training wheels. I discovered I couldn't when I crashed into the single garage door at the front of my child-hood home and busted my knee. It was the same knee I grazed when I was pushed over by a bully, and the same knee I picked at to secure Maddox's attention for five minutes at a time.

I cried when I picked at the scab enough to make it bleed, but Maddox and I almost always made it to the nurse's office at

Seaforth before one of his brother's arrived to chaperone the rest of our exchange.

The time alone with Maddox compensated for a scarred knee because I truly believed an ugly kneecap would be the worst thing I'd endure if my crush weren't reciprocated. I had no clue how naïve I was until my fascination with a Walsh family member reached my uncle's ears. He saw benefits in our friendship from the get-go, and he wasn't ashamed to announce them.

Regretfully for me, but also thankfully, my uncle wasn't the only one who noticed my year-long crush. Maddox's brothers were only a couple of years older than us, but they were mature enough to know the best way to protect their brother was to keep him as far away from me as possible. We were kept at arm's length since the day my uncle arrived to collect me from school instead of my mother, then the Walsh prolonged gawks occurred not long after that.

My thoughts return to the present—well, to the memories in my head in the present—when my mother's voice trickles into my ears. "Demi, why don't you go get Kaylee's blanket. It's a little chilly today."

Kaylee, I murmur to myself, certain I've heard the name before, but unsure why it stabs my heart with more pain than knowing I'll eventually wake from my dream, leaving my parents behind.

When my younger self leaps to her feet with a brisk nod of her head, instincts have me wanting to follow her, but for some reason, my feet remain rooted where they are. It's for the best. If I had gone with my instincts, I would have missed my mother ripping Kaylee out of my father's arm like her aggression didn't swap Kaylee's happy coos for wailing sobs. "Give her to me. You're spoiling her!"

After settling Kaylee's wails by tickling her feet, my father replies, "You can't spoil a baby, Monica. There's no such thing."

She *tsks* him as if she hates him. I'm surprised she has the gall. My dad was a gentle giant, but he still had the Petretti last name. That alone usually had people pulling into line.

I step back in shock when my mother sneers out, "You can when she isn't your child to ruin. You heard what he said. He could come back at any moment."

"I'm trying, Mon—"

My mother whips around so fast, Kaylee squeals like she's riding a rollercoaster. "You're not trying enough! You've *never* tried enough!" Her chest heaves as tears swamp her eyes. "If it weren't for him—"

"*Him.*" My father stands from his chair with an aggressive edge I never witnessed as a child. "*He* is the reason you were there. *He* almost took her away from you. *I* stopped him from doing that. *Me,* Monica. Yet you still hate me like I gave you away as easily as *he* did."

He removes a red-faced Kaylee from Mom's arms before placing her into a highchair butting against the kitchen table. With how much tension is hanging in the air, the last thing I anticipate my father to do is pull my mother into his arms. He dries her tears like her cruelness is excusable before he promises Mom that she made the right decision picking him.

My mother's tears are barely settled when my younger self re-enters the kitchen. My father is quick to remove the devastation from his face, but even my three-year-old self notices the change in his demeanor. Instead of moving for Kaylee to settle her whimpers with her favorite blankie or to hug my upset mother, she curls her arms around my daddy's thigh and burrows her head into his winter jacket.

When he bobs down to her level, his eyes are as gentle as the man I will forever remember. He stares like he truly loves her while silent promise after silent promise projects from his kind eyes. He pledged to protect my mother from being hurt again. Mine centers around me not being hurt to begin with.

I relish our little bubble of peace for five seconds before the heart-tugging scene fades to black like the movie in my head ran out of film.

I'm not left in the dark for long. Just as fast as the first scene faded, another one starts. This one is nowhere near as heartfelt as the previous one. My younger self is screaming blue murder while clawing her nails into my father's thigh.

"Daddy!" she cries on repeat when two men in long black coats attempt to wrench her away from him. They tug on her ankles, unrepentant that they're close to snapping her tiny bones. I'm older than I was in the last montage but only by a year or two.

The old brown couch in the middle of the room announces this is the living room of my childhood home, but the lack of worry on my mother's face would have you convinced other-wise. Her expression is neutral. Not even the slightest bit of gloss is seen in her eyes.

I can't say the same for my father. Even his lips quiver when he begs for the men to let me go. "Please. I'm begging you. She's a Petretti. She is mafia royalty. You can't do this."

My eyes dart to the corner of the room when a hand slices

through the air. Although the hand is covered by a leather glove perfect for hiding fingerprints, I know they belong to a man. Nothing occurs in this town unless it was a direct order given by the man who rules it.

My uncle has come to visit, but instead of arriving with gifts and splendor, he has come to maim.

"I told you what would happen if you disobeyed me, Sean." My brows furrow when my uncle steps out of the shadows. His face isn't as wrinkled as it was the last time I saw him, but the evilness in his eyes is abundant. "Despite your last name, you must pay for your error in judgment." He mockingly waves his hand over our much-loved yet derelict home. "You have nothing to give me that I don't already own…" My mother steps back when his eyes lock with hers for the briefest second, and he smiles an evil grin. "So I had to get inventive."

I want to fall to my knees and comfort the little girl clutching my dad's leg like he will forever be her hero when my uncle's focus shifts to her. She's so scared by his presence, she has peed her pants, and big salty blobs are streaming down her face unchecked.

It's clear she's traumatized enough she'll do everything in her power to push this exchange to the back of her mind the instant the horrifying event is over. Even more so when my uncle mutters in her ear, "You'll make a nice profit. Blonde hair and blue eyes went out of fashion years ago. They love milky white-skinned girls with dark, stormy hair. They'll pay top dollar for you."

"Leave her alone!" I scream at the same time my dad yanks my younger self behind him. My dad is taller than my uncle, and his shoulders are a tad wider, but since he was birthed by my grandfather's whore instead of his wife, he wasn't granted the notoriety my uncle has had since birth. The men lighting up his chest with semi-automatic weapons don't cower when he puffs his chest out with determination. They mock him, praying he will make a mistake that will leave them no choice but to break the rules their realm is governed by.

Much to his disgust, my uncle couldn't order the death of my father. However, he could torment him until he was nothing but a shell of skin and bones.

"Give her to me," my uncle snarls in my father's face, his closeness so near. Even with this memory being almost two decades old, I recall the ghastly scent that bounded out of his mouth. He drinks his liquor like he rules his monarch—hard and undiluted.

My father shakes his head before he adds a stern "No!" to his non-verbal reply.

My hand shoots up to clamp my mouth shut when my uncle backhands my father. He hits him so forcefully, a tooth clatters across the warped wooden floors of the living room. It's a hit that would see most men knocked out in an instant, but not my daddy. He remains standing tall, forever on guard when it comes to my mother and me.

"You're a fool, Sean," my uncle garbles out a short time later.

When my uncle clicks his fingers two times, I prepare my stomach for the worst. He only ever clicks his fingers when he's on a warpath with no intent for survivors.

My instincts are on point. Their focus was simply on the wrong child. The goons don't force themselves past my father to get to my younger self cowering behind his thigh. They snatch up the sleeping child in a crib at the side of the room. They take Kaylee.

"No!" my mother screams, her rebellion finally on par with my father's. "You promised," she screams on repeat while thumping her fists onto my uncle's chest. "You said she'd never be in any danger. That you would keep her safe."

My uncle's brutally swung fist ends her campaign for all of thirty seconds before she's back on her feet, yelling and hitting like she's possessed. But this time, her anger isn't fixed on my uncle. She hurls abuse at my father, telling him how she hates him and that she'll never forgive him.

She's so worked up she doesn't care that half of her wildly swung hits connect with my younger self instead of my father. She pummels into her on repeat, heartless to the fact my younger self's cries leave my father no choice but to shove her to the other side of the room with force.

When her head smashes into the wall with an *oomph,* my hand instinctively raises to the area my brain rattled against when my uncle hit me in his Audi. My head didn't crack the glass, but even weeks after his assault, a bump can still be felt under the skin.

While frantically trying to work out if this is a memory or a nightmare, I trace the lump. With my mother sobbing in the corner and my uncle and his goons gone with Kaylee, the house is eerily quiet. It replicates a house of horrors to perfection.

"It'll be okay, Demi. You know what mommy is like," my father mutters gently, drawing my focus back to him.

He lifts my younger self into his arms before he paces us toward my childhood bedroom. This time, I follow him, aware of who my focus needs to be on. I love my mother, but she was never there for me like my father was. That's why I was so surprised he killed himself. My uncle tormented him daily, but even during a mental psychosis, he chose to endure the torment than have it pushed onto me.

After changing my younger self's soiled pajamas, he places her into bed like his entire world isn't being upended before his very eyes, then carefully removes the locks stuck to her tear-drenched cheeks. Once he has them tucked behind her ears, he drags the tip of his index finger down her nose, raising her sagging lips into a ghost-like smile. "It's time to go to sleep now, Demi, but we'll make pancakes in the morning. Pancakes make everything better."

When he hums a familiar nursery rhyme, the memory in my head fades to another. This one appears to be a couple of years later than the first two. My knee is badly scarred, and the love hearts I drew over my schoolbooks have the same set of initials in them—MW.

The crib in the living room is gone, and a highchair no longer dangles off the end of the kitchen table. I could say that's because Kaylee would be too old for baby things, but my gut won't allow me to act so stupidly. Family photographs no longer adorn the fridge, and not an ounce of love is felt in the air. Not even the fake, made-up kind I didn't realize was fraudulent until now. It's cold and icy, and I appear more grateful that summer holidays are over than disappointed.

"Are you ready, kiddo?" my father asks as he walks into the kitchen. His shoulders appear heavier than they were in the last montage, but his large frame hides it well. "If you want the pick of the dorms, we better get a wiggle on."

He tickles my younger self's stomach like I did Kaylee's in the first memory before he gathers her school bag off the kitchen table. When he peers at my mother at the side of the room, it's obvious he'd give anything in the world to see her smile. He still loves her even with it appearing as if his love isn't reciprocated.

When she fails to notice his prolonged watch after several heart-wrenching seconds, he sighs, spins on his heels, then directs our trek outside. My younger self doesn't say goodbye to my mother either. It was rare to get a response out of her anyway. If my memory isn't leading me astray, she only said happy birthday to me the month prior. My party was six months earlier.

After climbing into the front seat of my father's run-down car, my younger self latches her seat belt, then peers into the back seat, exhaling harshly when she notices the back seat is void of a car seat.

"What happened to Kaylee?" I ask at the same time my younger self works up the courage to do the same.

My dad rustles her hair like he always did when he needed me to be quiet before he shifts the gearstick into park and drives away.

I stand in the driveway of my family home for the next several minutes. This area of Hopeton is rougher than the neighborhood my uncle lives in, but it has an appreciation for family pride. The lawns are maintained, and several children's toys are set up in the driveways for the neighborhood kids to use. It has a sense of community—a perception that is lost when a familiar-looking SUV pulls to the curb in the front of my family home.

When the back-passenger door pops open, and a suit-covered leg curls out, I twist to face the house, preparing to tell my mother to seek cover since my father isn't here to protect her from my uncle.

My warning falls short when I spot her kneeling in the doorway of my childhood home. The dowdy nightie she was picking lint balls off in the kitchen only minutes ago has been replaced with a silky negligee, and her once-unbrushed hair is flowing down her chest like a golden waterfall, unknotted and silky.

It dawns on me why I'm recalling this memory when my uncle's stalk up the cracked footpath of my family home is quickly followed by my father's truck pulling into the driveway. We forgot my suitcase full of my belongings, so we had to turn around to get it.

I watch the scene unfold as if it's the first time I'm witnessing it—the shouts of my father, the wailing screams of my mother, then the sheer terror on my father's face when he bolts out of the front door bloodied and banged up to tell my younger self to run.

"Run, Demi! Run!" he screams at the top of his lungs, sending my heart into a frenzy. "I'll find you. I promise. Just run."

As my younger self flings off her seat belt, two goons in the front of my uncle's car do the same. Instead of charging for my father, who looks like he's been in a scuffle, they race toward my younger self frozen partway out of my father's car.

"Run!" I scream to myself, truly unsure in my muddled state if she makes it out of the carnage alive.

You can live without a soul.

My mother is living proof of this.

With my heart in my throat and my head on lockdown, I watch the dark-haired girl run and run and run, my attention only diverting when my name is shouted in the direction opposite to where she's running.

It didn't come from my father, who is holding back my uncle like he won't feel the sting of his wrath almost instantaneously, nor from the neighbors watching the charade unfold with concern slashed across their features. It came from a bright white light at the end of the driveway.

It isn't a voice I recognize, but they're adamant they're not giving up. "Go again. We're not giving up. She's been on this table for hours, but she can beat this."

Forever curious, I step closer to the light. I make it almost halfway there when a brutal surge rocketing through my body folds my knees out beneath me. It's so painful, I'm tempted to stay here in the shelter of my memories. My dad is here, and he'll protect me no matter what, but for some reason unbeknownst to me, I crawl toward the light instead, certain the people calling my name need me more than the ghost of my dad.

The closer I get to the gaping hole, the more my memories shift from ones of my past to ones of my present—the teeny tiny little freckles dotted across Maddox's nose, his insanely sexy grin when he's thinking immorally wicked thoughts, and the way he says, "I love you back," instead of "I love you too," lowers the pain surging through me until it's barely a blip on the radar. I feel at peace like Maddox is the only person on the earth capable of making the pains of my past worthwhile.

Just before I'm swallowed by rays brighter than the sun, I

crank my neck back to my dad. He's no longer wrestling with my uncle. He's alone, standing in the doorway of my family home with a touch of a smile curving his lips. He mouths that he loves me before he nudges his head to the light, encouraging me to fall into a comfort as warm as his hugs once were.

3

MADDOX

My knee bobs up and down as I drop my eyes to my watch for the third time over the past twenty minutes. Demi has been in surgery for hours, and I've not had a single update about her condition. My patience is wearing thin. I would have charged into the OR and demanded an update hours ago if Saint didn't know me as well as he does. He's been glued to my right for the past six hours. Caidyn has taken up the left for almost as long.

Dr. Falgar suggested for Dr. Avery to call Demi's family. My family is as far as her calls went. Saint was with Sloane, so that made up for Demi's friends, and considering her family sees her as more of a commodity than an asset, I didn't bother updating them.

Col wouldn't shed a tear about the death of his niece. From what I heard, he smirked at his own brother's funeral. He doesn't deserve to be updated. He can rot in hell for all I care, and his son isn't too far behind him. If I hadn't been running drugs for Dimitri, I would have been with Demi, and she wouldn't have bled out on the bathroom floor of the cabin, unable and incapable of reaching out for help.

I fucked up, and karma is gnawing my ass for it.

My eyes pop up from my bloody hands when Caidyn squeezes my shoulder, announcing the arrival of Dr. Falgar. He isn't alone. A second doctor has joined him, making the total number of doctors in the OR waiting room at Mercer Private three. Dr. Avery is here too. She isn't here as a shrink this time around. She's here as a friend.

When my endeavor to read the expression on Dr. Falgar's face fails, I stand to my feet. He heads my way, but his eyes float over everyone in the room. The only person missing from my immediate family is Justine. Since we're unsure which way the chips will fall, my brothers and I decided that keeping her out of the Ravenshoe slash Hopeton area is best for all involved, especially since her 'dates' with Dimitri are still being investigated.

"Where is Demi's family?"

"We *are* her family," Sloane interrupts Dr. Falgar, her tone unforgiving.

Even aware that isn't true, the Petretti name is highly recognizable around these parts, Dr. Falgar jerks up his chin before gesturing for us to move to the side of the room for privacy.

I follow through with his request, as does the rest of my family. "Demi bled so profusely during her miscarriage because she had a blood condition known as Von Willebrand disease. It is usually a hereditary disease that causes issues with blood clotting. However, I believe Demi acquired it from another medical condition." He licks his lips before speaking a bunch of mumbo jumbo I don't understand. "Demi had a heart condition known as AV fistulas."

"Which is?" Caidyn asks at the same time my mother fists my father's shirt in a determined hold.

Dr. Falgar directs his eyes to Caidyn. "It is where arteries from her heart connect directly with the veins in her uterus and cervix. The pregnancy was *extremely* dangerous for her. It caused high-output heart failure due to renal arteriovenous fistula. Her heart couldn't take it. The damage was too significant."

While shaking my head, I take a step back, certain he isn't saying what I think he's saying. He is talking about Demi in past tense like she's no longer here.

"Where is she?" I push past my brothers, determined to make it to the door no matter how hard they strive to hold me down. "I want to see her."

"She didn't make it through surgery. We did everything we could."

"Where is she!" I scream into Dr. Falgar's face, my world crumbling as effectively as my legs when my brothers drag me to the floor.

I fight them with everything I have, uncaring of our mother's begs for us not to fight. My heart is breaking, shattered into a million pieces. I can't come back from this.

"Demi!" I punch, bite, and scream, then I call her name for the second time. "Demi!"

After stabbing my fingers under Saint's ribs, I push Caidyn off me before I spring to my feet and bolt for the door, sidestepping Landon on my way. I almost make it to the corridor when the one man who can stop me with only words steps into my path. My dad's face is shattered, he is as devastated as me, but his heart breaks even more when he pulls his youngest son's wet face into his chest to hold him while he cries.

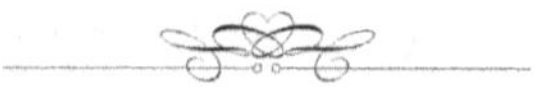

Shoes. Who would have thought something so insignificant was a requirement on your darkest day? When Caidyn packed my belongings, he packed *everything*, unsure if Demi and I would ever return to Ravenshoe. The knowledge saw my mother requesting for us to pop by the cabin on the way home. She doesn't want me walking into the funeral home shoeless, unaware my feet aren't the only part of me barren.

The cavity in my chest is just as bare.

"Do you want to take anything else?" Saint asks from his station near the bedroom door. A packed-in-a-hurry suitcase is in one of his hands, and a pair of polished dress shoes is in the other. "I can come back later and grab the rest. Sloane will help—"

I halt his offer with a brisk shake of my head. "I don't need *any* of this."

There was only one thing I wanted in this cabin.

She's no longer in it.

My steps to the front door slacken when a memory pops into my head for the briefest moment. I barely had the chance to give them the shock they deserved because I stumbled onto an almost unconscious Demi only a second later.

"Head out. I'll join you in a minute."

Saint immediately shakes his head. "Madd—"

"I don't need a fucking shadow, Saint. A shadow won't bring

her back. *Nothing* will bring her back." I ball my hands into fists, choosing anger over grief. "I just want a fucking minute to wrap my head around this. Just a moment of peace. Can you not give me that, Sebastian? Can you not think about what *I* need for a change?"

"This has *always* been about you, Maddox. *All* of it."

He doesn't say it, but I know he's remorseful for how long he kept Demi and me apart even with him having a reason to gloat. This is *exactly* what he predicted.

A heartbreak like nothing else.

Pure fucking devastation.

"If you can't see that, then you're more blind than even I realized."

After tossing over a stack of drawers like they're weightless, he pivots on his heels and stalks away. I hate that I made him upset, but my devastation is too perverse to fix all the mistakes I've made right now. My mind is elsewhere, where it should have been all along.

A rattling breath parts my lips when I lower the bathroom door handle. Even with her leaving the bathroom hours ago, Demi's scent lingers in the air. It's a subtle smell that reminds me of long walks in the wilderness followed by a hefty helping of cranberry pie. It's sweet and addictive, a brutally horrifying reminder of just how much I've lost.

The pain in my chest is intense. I'm shocked I can function through it. However, it has nothing on the grief that rips through me when I stop in front of the very things responsible for the intermission in my grief. Three little white sticks are lined up in a row. They're all positive, but they aren't wonky like they were placed down by a shaky hand. They're in an exact line, as symmetrically perfect as the woman who took them.

Their careful placement exposes Demi wasn't devastated by the news she was going to become a mother. She was happy about the prospect. I'm so confident in my assessment, I truly believe even if she knew how much danger she'd face to carry my child, she still would have gone through with the pregnancy.

She was fearless like that.

Incapable of being taken down.

The strongest woman I've ever known.

And now she is gone.

My grief is already at a pinnacle, so you can imagine how far it soars when I catch the quickest glimpse of red embedded in the shower stall floor. Most of Demi's blood has circled down the drain. Only the slightest bit of evidence of the devastation that occurred here today is stuck in the white grout. It's bloody and red, as gory as the coloring that ran from my knuckles when I scrubbed them with a grout cleaner with the hopes of removing Igor's blood from my hands.

I killed a father, and now the woman I love was killed before she could make me a father. In a sick, twisted way, it makes sense. Evil is like a boomerang. It always comes back faster, harder, and more devastatingly.

With my heartbreak at a pinnacle, I kick out without thinking, too distraught to consider the consequences of my action. My recently booted-up foot breaks through the glass surrounding the shower stall. The shards digging into my calves should slow me down, but it hardly makes an indent to a man pummeled with grief.

After stepping over the glass spanning one half of the bathroom, I set to work on remodeling the tiles in the stall with my fists. I punch and punch and punch the gleaming white material until my knuckles bust open, and I'm on my knees, shuddering and blubbering like I'm on the verge of a breakdown.

I lost the woman I love and my child on the same day.

Not even He-Man couldn't act unaffected by such a devastating blow.

When the sound of glass crunching under shoes trickles through my ears, I anticipate being wrapped up by one of my brothers and carted out of the cabin like I was forcefully removed from Mercer Private an hour ago, so you can imagine my shock when I'm left to handle my grief alone for the next several minutes.

After dragging my hand under my nose to remove the contents pooled there, I angle my head just enough to spot the person eyeballing me but maintaining an amicable distance. An ill-timed chuckle leaves my mouth when the eyes peering back at me aren't close to the coloring my family was gifted. They have a green edge to them like Justine and me, but not an ounce of blue is associated with them. Rocco Shay's eye coloring doesn't alter depending on his mood. They only have two settings—murderer and remorseful. Today they appear to have a bit of both.

"What did the wall ever do to you?" While licking his lips, he pinches his jeans, loosening up the stiff material, before he bobs down in front of me. His movements are brisk, but I don't miss the quickest straying of his eyes to the pregnancy tests on the vanity sink. "Having a bad day, are we?" Although he's asking a question, he doesn't wait for me to reply. "Probably not as bad as mine. You were three bricks short, then you failed to return the Buick. What if I had another run organized for this afternoon? What would have happened to me then?" He *tsks* me like the past eight hours were nothing but a nightmare. "You're lucky I like your girl, Ox, or I would have added your brain matter to the bloodstains in the shower."

Is he fucking kidding me? Demi is dead, yet all he's worried about is a couple of pounds of coke.

With my anger too perverse to ignore, I grab Rocco by the throat, stand us to our feet, then pin him to the shower now housing several cracked tiles. He could fight me. He's a little taller than me and around the same weight, but he's too busy laughing to respond to my aggression.

That's all set aside when I scream in his face, "Demi is dead, you fuckin' piece of shit. So if you think I give a shit about some missing bricks, you're dead fucking wrong. I hope you burn in hell, the whole fucking lot of you."

"Hold up. Go back. What the fuck are you saying?"

I glare at him as if to say, *how can I make it any more obvious for you?*

I straight up told him what happened. I can't put it any more bluntly.

After forcefully removing himself from my hold, then taking a couple of seconds to deliberate, Rocco locks his eyes with mine. "Did you see her body?"

I huff out an annoying grunt before moving to the sink to gather up the pregnancy tests I plan to take with me. "This wasn't a mob hit."

Even if you're not in the mob, you'd still be aware the Petrettis don't leave a body, and although I'd love someone to blame but myself, this time around, Demi's death only falls on one set of shoulders. *Mine.*

"That wasn't what I asked." Rocco stops me from leaving the bathroom by pinching the muscle between my shoulder and neck.

Unlike him, I retaliate to his aggressive stance with violence.

He doesn't laugh this time around. He uses words instead. "If you ain't seen a body, you should *never* believe someone is dead. Been played a trick or two on before. Won't happen again."

I pull him forward by the collar of his shirt before slamming him backward. "Speak fucking English, Rocco. I don't have time for your shit."

Even though he's smiling, I know he wants to pummel my words back into my mouth with his fists. His narrowed gaze is very telling. "Since you seem to have trouble understanding me, how about I show you what I mean?"

Not waiting for me to answer, he pushes me away from him, almost sending me toppling onto my ass before he digs his phone out of his pocket.

"No fucking way," I grunt out in disbelief when he brings up a photo of Ophelia Petretti. I'm not talking about one when she was young and wild. If the kid with identical lips and eyes wrapped around her leg is anything to go by, she settled down after her 'death.'

"Do you understand me now, Ox? Or should I write it down for you?" Rocco asks while pretending to write a note on his hand.

I doubt he will have the possibility of writing anything when Dimitri unearths what he's hiding. I don't claim to know

Dimitri's inner-workings, but the grief he displayed when they lowered his sister's casket into the ground wasn't fake. He's a hard-ass gangster, but not even the world's best actor could portray the set of emotions that hit him that day. It was a perfect representation of the expression that was projected back at me when I looked in the vanity mirror only minutes ago. He was beyond devastated.

"Attaboy, get on your bike," Rocco pushes out with a laugh when it dawns on me what I must do. Landon doesn't believe anything presented to him without evidence, and neither the fuck do I, so I have no clue why I went off-script today.

When my sprint through the front door of the cabin converts Rocco's whipping noises to faint rustles of the wind, I realize why my breakdown in the bathroom went unannounced to my family. The cabin must be soundproof. I can barely hear Rocco's chuckles, and he sounds like a hyena when he really gets going.

"Maddox," Caidyn growls in a warning tone when he spots the determination on my face. "Think about this."

He tries to beat me to my bike. It's unfortunate for him, suaveness doesn't count when it comes to physical fitness. I throw a leg over my ride and kick out the start lever before he's within touching distance of me, and even quicker than that, my despair switches to hope.

My dad commands the road like he commands the air when he's flying, but not even his racecar-driver-inspired skills will have him reaching Mercer Private before me. I can maneuver my bike between cars. My father can only go around them.

"You can't park here," a security guard with thick biceps and tattooed hands grunts out when I skid my bike to a stop at the front of the hospital eighteen minutes later. "This is a restricted area."

My determination to sidestep him grows when I notice a familiar-looking vehicle parked in the 'police, fire, and ambulance only' bay.

The Lincoln's plates aren't local.

They rarely are when it comes to the FBI.

"Sir…" The deep baritone of the security guard's voice is gobbled up by the squeak of a nurse when I dart through the rapidly closing doors of the elevator cart, of which, she is the sole occupant.

"What floor is the morgue?" I ask, my tone low from watching the security guard alerting other officers to my presence via the walkie-talkie curled over his shoulder.

Even with my hope higher than it's ever been, wrangling underpaid security personnel isn't my main priority. What if Rocco is wrong? What if there is a body, and I simply failed to ask to see it? It is plausible.

The last image I want in my head is of Demi lying on a cold and sterile gurney. The vision of her slumped in the shower isn't any better, but we had many good memories in there I could mix it with to make it seem not as devastating as it was.

I put my private contemplations onto the back burner when the nurse steps closer to me. Her eyes are kind, but they're also brimming with mischievousness. "We don't have a morgue here. Patients are transferred to Ravenshoe each evening."

I curse under my breath before backing it up with a voiced one. "Fuck!"

My profanity doesn't bother the nurse. If anything, it makes her more sympathetic to my cause. "From what I heard, that doesn't occur until after midnight. If this was a recent passing, she could still be here." The fact she said 'she' reveals she's an old romantic at heart. "They keep them on the ward they were assigned during admission until transport is organized. Do you know which ward she was on?"

I nod so briskly I make myself woozy. "The surgical ward."

After pushing the button for the seventh floor, the nurse commences removing her navy blue smock. "Sorry," she apologizes with a smile when she accidentally bumps into me. "It's been a very long shift. I'm dead on my feet."

My eyes shift from the impish pair staring at me to the elevator panel above our heads when it dings only a second later. We've reached the second level, the nurse's apparent desired floor.

"Good luck. I hope you find her in time," she says while walking out of the elevator cart.

I lose the chance to reply when she races for the stairwell. Through the glass walls of the elevator cart that looks out over the garden atrium in the center of the hospital, I watch her gallop down the single flight of stairs we rode together. When she reaches the foyer, she discards her smock into a waste receptacle in the middle of the bustling space before she spins around to face me. My mouth gapes when she jangles my bike key in the air, clear as day for me to see. I'm unsure whether I should laugh or cry that I got pickpocketed by a con artist in a nurse's uniform. If it were any other day than today, I'd respond to her gall. Since it isn't, I act oblivious to the familiar rumble of my motorbike's engine when it's being pushed to its limits.

I'm so stunned by the turn of events, a man leaning against an IV stand asks me three times if I'm going up or down before

I register that he is talking to me. "This place isn't a bore-fest, but surely you've got better things to do than ride the elevator for fun?" His toothy grin exposes there's no malice in his tone, much less his frail clutch of his IV stand. "If not, I'm more than happy to cruise with you, but can we take a detour to the rooftop? This place is going into lockdown within the hour." He raps his frail fingers against the cigarette packet in his hands. "Last time that happened, I was locked in my room for hours. The window doesn't open, and the head of nursing is a fucking hardass." His eyes gleam like he's way off the mark with his comment about the head nurse. "The good ones always are, aren't they?"

I jerk up my chin before stepping out of the elevator, finally clueing on to the fact the elevator stopped because it reached my desired floor.

With my boorish demeanor announcing I'm not up for a chit-chat, the man I'd guess to be mid-fifties shuffles into the elevator cart before pressing the button for the rooftop. Just before the doors shut with him on the other side, the rational half of my brain switches back on.

I jab my arm between the gleaming metal doors, stopping their closure. The brown-eyed man startles, but the wires and cables protruding out of his body assure me an inquisitive mind is the least of his problems.

"Did they mention what the lockdown was about?"

He shakes his head. "This isn't my first rodeo. I've slept here more times than in my own bed the past couple of years, but I learned early on not to ask questions if I want lung disease to be the cause of death on my death certificate." His tongue delves out to lick his nicotine-stained lips while his eyes rake my body.

I don't know what he sees, I feel more broken than complete, but it once again has the chips falling in my favor. "For what it's worth, most of the commotion today came from the west wing."

"The west wing?" I double-check, wanting to ensure the frantic beat of my heart doesn't have me mistaking what he said.

He lifts his chin for the second time. "Take a left once you go through the double doors of the surgical unit. The west wing is at the end of the corridor." When I release the doors so he can relish in the addiction that's slowly killing him, he warns, "Keep your head down low. They're *always* watching."

I issue my thanks with a dip of my head before breaking through the double doors he mentioned. After taking a sharp left, I tuck my chin in close to my chest. Even a man with a dead-cold heart would feel the heat of several motion-activated cameras on him. They have a way of restarting even heartless men's hearts.

My already cautious steps slow even more when a male voice sounds through my ears. It isn't what the Russian says two doors up from me that has me paying careful attention. It's who he's talking about.

My name is mentioned several times in a row.

"Why would she take his bike? That won't improve matters! *Она испортит мне всю операцию.*"

I push off my feet with a roar when the beep of a cell phone being shutdown is chased by the Russian voice demanding for the floor to be placed into immediate lockdown. I sprint past the office he's commanding so fast, I'm certain I am nothing but a blur, but regretfully, rogue agents are more watchful than their younger, more strait-laced counterparts.

"Maddox!" My name scarcely leaves Agent Brahn's mouth when the thud of his boots boom into my ears. He's on my tail in an instant, and even faster than that, I'm crash tackled by two plain-clothed security officers I didn't see coming from the other direction.

"Let me go! It's my right to see her!"

I fight them with more gusto than I did my brothers, unforgiving if I hurt them. Even if the hope fueling my campaign the past thirty minutes is completely false, they're denying me the chance to say a final goodbye to Demi. That, in itself, deserves retribution.

"Get off me! I want to see Demi! It's my right to see her!"

I fight and fight and fight until the faintest trickle of a voice I wouldn't forget in a million years stops my crusade in an instant. "Maddox?"

4

DEMI

Maddox stares at me as if I am a ghost. Excluding the frantic thrust of his chest, he lays completely still, motionless and unmoving. His response to seeing me up and out of bed after a three-hour-long operation shocks me until recognition for his distress dawns on me.

With my jaw tight with annoyance, I shift my focus to the tall Russian agent at the back of the pack. "I said no!"

I had barely come to from an emergency D&C when I was propositioned with a wildly eccentric plan to have me permanently ostracized from the Petretti family. Agent Brahn was going to tell Maddox I didn't make it through my surgery, that I had a condition that made it fatal for me to fall pregnant.

Years ago, I would have accepted his offer without the slightest bit of hesitation. Today, the only reply that formulated in my head was a stern no. I couldn't leave Maddox, not in a million years, so there was no way I would leave him by making out he was partly responsible for my demise. It takes two to tango, just like it takes two to make a baby. Once Maddox's grief had lessened, guilt would have taken over.

That alone had me explicitly stating to Agent Brahn numerous times during our thirty-minute conversation this morning that I would never go through with his plan. I thought I made myself perfectly clear. Clearly, I need more practice at exerting my authority, and now is as good a time as any. "You said it was my choice! That you'd never force me to do anything against my wishes."

Agent Brahn steps toward me with his hands held out like my father did anytime memories of my past resurfaced the nightmares I was plagued with for most of my childhood. He had a way of making me forget the bad times and cherish the good. "Motions were put into play before you woke. I've never had an offer turned down before, so—"

"You told him I was dead? That I died on the operating table?"

Needing confirmation to my questions from the only man I trust, I lower my eyes to Maddox pinned to the floor by two agents. The torment in his voice when he screamed to see me already endorses my claims, not to mention the absolute despair still dampening the usually bright gleam in his eyes.

He thought I was dead.

That hurts me almost as much as knowing our baby is gone.

When I speak, my voice cracks, strangled by the remorse clutching my throat. "I'm so sorry."

"You have *nothing* to be sorry for, Demi. Nothing at all," Maddox promises, his voice unlike anything I've ever heard. "Nothing happening is your fault."

When recognition of the last time he spoke those words to me filter through my head, three little tears topple down my cheeks.

He was there.

He found me.

Oh, God. I can only imagine how painful that was for him.

The expression on Maddox's face reveals how badly he wants to wipe away my tears, and he is given the chance when Agent Brahn signals for the undercover agents to let him go. But instead of removing them in shame, he gives them meaning by locking our lips together.

After telling me he loves me, he kisses me like I've never been kissed before. It is an embrace so blinding, even with my insides feeling like they're being pulled in different directions, I loosen my grip of the IV stand before weaving my fingers through his thick locks to secure his mouth to mine.

If I had it my way, I'd stay here for eternity. Regretfully, Agent Brahn has other ideas. His cough is subtle but loud enough for me to get the hint that Maddox and I are gaining an audience, so with reluctance, I pull back from Maddox's blistering embrace.

"I'm so sorry," I express again when I see the sheer devastation still lingering in his hooded gaze. "I told them no," I whisper over his kiss-swollen mouth before nibbling on his lower lip a little more, forever craving more when it comes to him. "I would have never gone through with their plans. I would *never* hurt you like that."

Maddox bites on my bottom lip, drags his tongue across the sting, then delves it back into my mouth. The saltiness of my tears flavors our kiss for the next several minutes. We have an audience. I can feel the eyes of a dozen people on us, but I don't care. When Maddox's lips are on mine, the world fades away. It is just him—my knight in shining armor—and me.

"Not yet," Maddox murmurs against my lips when I pull back for a quick breather. "I thought I'd lost the opportunity to do this. I need more. Lots *lots* more."

After scooping me into his arms like we're not being eyeballed by patients dying for their daily dose of drama, Maddox's greedy tongue slices through the giggle rumbling in my chest. I'm in a town bordering the one my uncle reigns, in the hospital where our unborn child lost its life, yet I feel like the luckiest woman on the planet.

It is crazy for me to feel this way. It has me worried I'm mentally unstable, but it's also understandable. When I woke up alone hours ago, I thought I had lost more than my child, so discovering that isn't the case is worth celebrating. I'll most likely regret it when guilt settles in, but for now, I'm going to cherish it.

With one hand on my ass, holding me in place, Maddox curls the other around my IV stand, then walks us in the direction the agents sprinted from before they tackled him. My repentance arrives earlier than expected when he mutters partway down, "You scared me." His tone hints at the double meaning of his comment. He was terrified long before Agent Brahn orchestrated a horrifying ruse to pull the wool over his eyes.

After rubbing at the deep groove between his brows with my thumb, I assure him, "That was *never* my intention. I thought a shower would calm everything down. It appears to have made things worse."

I'm still at a loss as to what happened this morning at the cabin. I remember entering the shower stall and rejoicing how the hot water reduced the pain of the sudden onset of cramps I was facing, but from there, the rest of my morning is pretty much blank. I didn't recall how I got to the hospital until Maddox returned fragments of my memories only minutes ago, and the reason for my visit didn't come to light until I woke up in recovery surrounded by unfamiliar faces.

After bouncing his wet eyes between mine enough times to make me dizzy, Maddox asks the one question I'd give anything to answer differently. "Our baby?"

Two little words shouldn't say so much, but when they're expressed by a man in the throes of grief, they could fill the pages of a book.

Apologies sit on the tip of my tongue, but before they spill, I realize I have nothing to be sorry for. Despite wishing otherwise, miscarriages occur all the time. I will forever wish our baby had beat the odds, but I learned a long time ago you can't always have what you wish for.

After ensuring Maddox has seen the remorse in my eyes, I say, "Dr. Falgar said we can try again when ready." The annoyance darting through Maddox's eyes has me confident my next set of words need to be shared. "But I'm happy to wait until the timing is right. We're new, so why not enjoy being 'us' for a little bit longer?"

"Is that what you want, Demi? Because if that is what you want, I'll wait until you're ready." His drenched eyes are brimming with both optimism and devastation. "But if it isn't, I'm okay with that as well." He smiles at my bug-eyed expression before he nudges his head to the empty suite at the end of the west wing, wordlessly questioning if it is my room.

When I nod, his interrogation delves a little deeper into the murkiness that kept us apart longer than we've been the past seven weeks. "What else did Dr. Falgar tell you?"

He places me onto the bed, plugs my IV back into the power switch like he was destined to be a medic before pulling up the bedding so that it maintains my modesty from the three agents watching our every move from the corridor outside of my room.

I take a minute to recall my brief conversation with Dr. Falgar before we were interrupted by Agent Brahn. "He said I have a blood clotting condition." My eyelids rapidly blink as I strive to recall the name of the hereditary condition I have. "It started with a V?"

"Von Willebrand disease?" Maddox's tone is clipped but also curious. Although it's rare to see him angry, his angst isn't focused on me, so I find it more endearing than upsetting.

I answer Maddox's question with a nod, unsure I can speak without squeaking. I shed many tears over the loss of our baby and almost just as many when I thought I had to wade through the grief alone. Abandonment isn't a Walsh trait, but the last couple of days were rocky for us, so I was weary Maddox's understanding might have been stretched thin.

I should have known better.

While tracing the veins in my hand with his thumb, backing up my claims his annoyance has nothing to do with me, Maddox asks, "Did he say anything about a heart condition?"

I barely move my head half an inch when a voice from

outside the room steals the last of Maddox's nerves. "Reporting that she had AV fistulas was my idea. I knew you wouldn't believe she had died because of a miscarriage, so I hatched something more convincing."

When Maddox mumbles, "You fucking son of a bitch," under his breath, I shoot my hand out to cover his balled one. I'm more than happy for him to exchange words with the man who caused him a world of pain, but I'd rather their conversation be nonphysical. I'll never have the chance of fully eradicating the groove between his brows if he's in lockup for assaulting a federal agent.

"I had to do something." Agent Brahn's voice is full of angst, but Maddox doesn't hear it. He's too angry to let a smidge of remorse weaken his campaign for vengeance. "If I hadn't, prior incidents left no doubt that she would be dead in under a month."

Maddox is quick to shut down the fear Agent Brahn's comment caused his face, but it does little to free his voice of alarm. "I had a handle on things."

Agent Brahn scoffs like his assurance isn't close to accurate. "Murder is *not* the solution for anything."

Maddox balks, but his lips remain tightly shut. That's more shocking than learning my fifteen-year crush was reciprocated.

Confident he has him where he wants him, Agent Brahn enters the room without the two shadows he's rarely without. I don't know the names of the blond agents forever at his side, but Agent Brahn is rarely seen without them. "You played into Col's hand when you arrived at the warehouse to fight."

"The warehouse your agency was meant to storm *long*

before I got near the ring," Maddox fires back, his reply a roar. "I had no choice but to take Igor down. If I hadn't killed him, he would have killed me."

The FBI was the reason Maddox was distracted the night he fought in the fight-until-the-death match. He was expecting help to arrive, unaware my uncle has as many law enforcement officers on his payroll as he does thugs.

When disbelief shoots through Agent Brahn's eyes, skeptical about Maddox's claims, I back Maddox up. "Maddox was wearing a wire. He dumped it into the waste bin outside of the bar you confronted me at. Why would he do that if he was on my uncle's side? If *any* of the men in attendance that night find out he was wearing a wire, his entire family will become extinct. Maddox wouldn't risk them for anyone." *Not even me.*

I wish I could say the medication hazing my mind is responsible for my eccentrics, but that's far from the truth. The Petrettis don't leave a body because they can talk. More times than not, grieving family members scream even louder than a corpse, so I am extremely confident about the last half of my statement.

Before I can add more credit to my claims, Maddox's next set of words pulls the earth out from beneath my feet. "Let me go with her." When confusion blasts through Agent Brahn's eyes, Maddox adds, "That's what you're planning, isn't it? To hide her away like you did Ophelia by convincing everyone she's dead?"

I don't know what shocks me more. Maddox's assumption that Ophelia is alive or the confirmation darting through Agent Brahn's eyes. It could be a combination of both.

A new type of shock numbs my heart when recollection of

the nightmare I had while under the influence of anesthetics slams into me. "Is that what you did with Kaylee? Did you hide her away too?"

"Kaylee?" Maddox and Agent Brahn query at the same time.

"My sister…" I stop truly unsure if it's trauma talking or me. "I think." I shake my head to clear the fog shrouding it. It is stupid of me to do. It hazes my mind more.

"Get the doctor."

"I'm okay," I assure Maddox, interrupting his race to the corridor with a gentle tap on his hand. "I'm just a little confused. I had a… *dream* while I was in the OR, except it didn't feel like a dream." I lick my lips before lowering my voice so it's only for Maddox's ears. "At the death-match, my uncle mentioned something about me having a sister, but with everything that had happened, I completely forgot about it."

"That's okay. It's understandable," he replies, forever reasonable. "Trauma has a way of messing with our heads."

"It does," I agree before I realize this is the perfect opportunity to guide Maddox through the darkness swamping him. "That's why you need to rethink your suggestion. You can't leave your family, Maddox. They'd never recover." I cup his jaw like we are once again the only two people in the world. "Think about what you went through when you thought I was gone. Do you truly want to put them through that?"

Maddox shakes his head in an instant, but he is as stubborn as a mule. "But we don't have any other options. If we stay, I'll soon become him."

His reply stumps me for all of two seconds. I forgot what week it is. His next death-match is this weekend. The first one indisputably changed him. I don't know if he will come out of a second one the same man.

I mull over our minimum choices for a couple of seconds before breathing heavily out of my nose. "Perhaps we should ask him for help?"

When I inconspicuously nudge my head to Agent Brahn, Maddox's head shake isn't as rapid as his first, but it eventually arrives. "We can't trust them. You know what Agent Moses is like." Nothing but pure disdain highlights his tone.

Although he kept the details minimal, I understand his dislike of Agent Moses. How could you not hate a man who forced you to become a murderer? I'm just fortunate Maddox doesn't blame me the same way.

I realize Agent Brahn has better hearing than a man his age should when he says, "We're not all like Agent Moses."

A gasp escapes my lips when my peer past Maddox's shoulder has me stumbling onto an empty corridor. The two blond agents are gone, and the door to my room has been shut to maintain privacy.

"All agents use the benefits that come from being a part of the Bureau. Most use them for good. Others…"

"Use it to fuck over the people they are meant to protect." Maddox's pitch announces he isn't asking a question. He's stating a fact. "Which category do you belong in, *Agent* Brahn?" The contempt his question is laced with exposes which team he believes Agent Brahn is on. It isn't ours. "Because from where I'm standing, your boots are just as muddy as Agent Moses's."

Agent Brahn smirks like Maddox isn't underhandedly calling him out as a rogue agent. "My boots are muddy because they were forced to trek through shit *neither of us* should be anywhere near." I feel like I missed the punch line when his comment makes Maddox's Adam's apple bob up and down. "Hiding one person is incredibly difficult. Two..." a whistle vibrates through Agent Brahn's thick lips, "... you'd have a better chance of winning the lotto. But when one of them is a criminal, you may as well send them to their enemies with a bullseye painted on their backs. They're all but dead."

I'm about to defend Maddox, to explain he wouldn't have killed Igor if he had any other choice, but Maddox stops my campaign by asking to have a word with Agent Brahn outside.

Usually, his chivalry would turn me on.

Today, it just pisses me off.

We're in a town bordering Hopeton, so my rights are about as thin as my patience is becoming, but I never anticipated having my opinion disregarded by Maddox. He, of all people, knows how important it is for victims to have a voice. His mother is an advocate for it. She boards the national domestic violence organization.

"You're not having a conversation in the hall like you aren't talking about me. This centers around me, so I'm going to be a part of the conversation."

A guilty mask slips over Maddox's face, but nothing halts his campaign. "Demi—"

"No, Maddox. If it weren't for me, you wouldn't be in this mess. Your family wouldn't hate me for forcing you to change who you are, and—"

"You'd most likely be dead in a ditch." Maddox's voice is filled with pure, adulterated angst. "Do you understand how much that guts me, Demi? How it plagues my nightmares more than Igor's last breath? I did what needed to be done to keep you safe, and I'll continue doing it until your uncle is either dead or you are free from him."

I've secretly loved Maddox for years, but today is the first time it's wholly consumed me. I'm speechless, both in awe and admiration. I knew what we had was special. The fact he went against everything he's ever believed in for me was a sure-fire sign of this, but I'm still stunned. I never thought I would come before his family. Not once.

Feeling the sentiment in the air as readily as me, Agent Brahn rejoins the conversation with a negotiation. "Moving two people is hard. It will take more time, more diligence, and more money."

"But?" Maddox and I ask at the same time, aware there's more to his interruption than a reminder about the impossible task we're hoping to pull off.

"But... it could be achievable if both parties are one hundred percent committed to the cause. This won't fall back on the Bureau if it fails. It will be *all* on us. If I bring them in, I risk my team being disbanded, and you risk having your location unearthed. From here on out, this must remain between the three of us. No third parties can be brought in. Do you understand?"

Maddox's nod is convincing.

I, however, need a couple more minutes to deliberate. "Can we think about it?"

The disappointment that darts through Maddox's eyes cut me like a knife. Thankfully, the gratitude I feel when Agent Brahn dips his chin makes the wound not as painful.

"I have a dozen matters to sort out before I can consider what our next step should be." Agent Brahn bounces his eyes between Maddox and me. For a tall man with wide shoulders, a shiny head, and an immorally corrupt smirk, his eyes reflect nothing but kindness. "Take the time. Use it wisely." He drops his eyes to Maddox's pocket that is vibrating like crazy. "And stay off that. Agent Machini moved your bike so we'd have a cover story if needed. If you alter her plan of attack, the first chip in the stack will commence wobbling. It only takes one wobble to spill an entire stack."

"I understand," Maddox says while pulling his cell phone out of his pocket to silence it. I can't see the screen of his phone, but I'm confident it is one of his brothers calling him. Unlike my family, they stick together through thick and thin.

After a final cautious grin, Agent Brahn exits my room, shutting the door behind him. I have every intention to use the time wisely as suggested, but it seems as if Maddox has other ideas. He requests for me to lay down before he toes off his nicked-up shoes, dumps them under the chair next to my bed, then asks me to scoot over.

The pain scuttling through my veins doubles when he joins me on my bed. He isn't hogging the mattress like he usually does. His eyes are responsible for the constrictive hold on my heart. The fluorescent tube lighting above our heads had me mistaking how green they are. Nearly all the blue is gone, leaving nothing but green flecks of torment, love, and heartbrokenness—three starkly contradicting emotions for one immensely intense pair of eyes.

"Maddox—"

"Not yet." He floats his eyes ever so slowly across my cheeks and down my nose until he stops at my lips. "I need more than a few minutes to drink in every perfect piece."

I nuzzle into the hand he uses to trace the scar on my right cheek, then I breathe heavily into his palm when he treks his thumb across my lips. "Tell me I'm not dreaming. That I didn't get into a wreck on my race back to the hospital."

Even with my confusion at a pinnacle, I reply, "You're not dreaming."

I was unaware he had left the hospital. I hated waking up alone and confused as to what had happened, but I assumed Maddox was close by. That he needed a minute to wrap his head around the fact we were going to be parents before our child was cruelly stripped away from us—kind of how Kaylee was from my parents.

I try to keep the focus on the future instead of the past, but that is hard to do when selfishness isn't naturally ingrained like it is with my uncle. "He said he killed my sister."

Maddox appears lost about the swift change in our conversation, but he catches on remarkably quick. It doesn't take a genius to unearth who is responsible for the furious heat burning me alive from the inside out. I've never disliked a single person I've met because the hate I have for my uncle leaves no room for anyone else.

"I think I was three or four at the time. Kaylee was young." While trudging through the mess of an anesthetic hazed brain, I seek one of the tiny freckles dotted across Maddox's chest. If my memories aren't leading me astray, I did the same thing anytime my brain sorted answers to questions a child should never need to ask. "I think she was around two… if that. Her hair was lighter than mine." I smile when a memory I hid many years ago pushes through the fog clouding me. "Dad said that was because her halo was still above her head. I had supposedly ripped mine off years earlier with the tenacity of a bull shark."

Although the vibration trembling in Maddox's chest exposes he found my comment as humorous as I did, he keeps his chuckles on the down-low. There's too much guilt in my voice for him to portray happiness.

"I can't believe I forgot her."

Maddox tucks a loose strand of hair behind my ear before raising my chin so we're eye to eye. "Don't be so hard on yourself. You said you were three or four. I struggle remembering what happened last week."

He has a point, but that's only because all the evidence hasn't been presented just yet. "I asked about Kaylee when I was seven. Dad kept a baby seat in the back of his truck for years, then one day it was gone." When I shake my head, incapable of conveying my shock that my father kept something so vital from me, a rogue tear falls down my cheek. It doesn't fill me with shame like it usually would. I'm too horrified that I am mourning the loss of my sister many years after her death to feel something as worthless as embarrassment. "Why did he keep her a secret from me? Why did he act like she never existed?"

"I don't know," Maddox answers, genuinely stumped for a better reply. "But from what you've shared about your father, he did it for a reason, Demi. To protect you. To keep *you* safe. He didn't do it to hurt you. You have to believe that."

The words he is speaking are true. My daddy loved me like no man ever had before Maddox, but it still hurts knowing he took a critical part of my life and made out as if she wasn't important. I had a sister, someone I could have looked out for and protected like Maddox does his siblings, yet I completely forgot about her until my own life precariously floated in the wind.

That makes me a terrible person.

It makes me unworthy of love.

"No, Demi," Maddox says sternly when I attempt to pull back. "You promised that you wouldn't run when you get scared."

"I'm not scared. I am…" My words trail off when I fail to find a reason for my stupid, unhinged behavior.

"Angry?" Maddox asks as his massively dilated eyes bounce between mine. "Mad? Wishing like fuck you could treat your uncle as poorly as he's treated you?"

"Yes!" I shout on a sob. "I hate him. Who he is. Who he made me be. What he made you do." Tears trickle down my cheeks when I stammer out, "A-And our b-baby. Despite him claiming otherwise, he can't perform miracles, but I can't help but blame him for that too. If he hadn't made us so stressed, maybe I would still be pregnant."

My heart pains when Maddox remains quiet while removing the salty blobs from my face. He did the same thing when I cried in his arms for the first time because he'd rather remain quiet than lie.

I swore back then I'd never let my uncle get the best of me again.

I didn't even last two damn months.

"I'm sorry. I am being ridiculous. It must be the hormones."

Maddox shakes his head. "You're not ridiculous, stupid, or hormonal. You are *mourning*." He scoots in so close we breathe as one. "Your sister and our baby, your life before your dad died. It may not have always been sunny, but it deserves to be acknowledged, and you deserve to grieve your loss." He presses his lips to my mouth before he uses them to clear away the wetness on my cheeks. He doesn't kiss away my tears. The words that spill from his mouth make me feel so loved, the surge of blood through my heart instantly dries them. "Nothing you could say, do, or feel could ever be ridiculous. It matters because *you* matter, Demi. You have always mattered. To your dad, to Sloane, to my family…" he saves the best for last, "…to me."

My head bob is feeble, but for the first time in my life, I have faith in my reply. I will never cure cancer nor will I land a rocket on the moon, but it isn't just geniuses who play a role in our community. We all have a part to play. It's just up to us to determine how impacting it will be.

After chuckling to hide his shock about how quickly I agreed with his statement, Maddox pulls me into his chest. A short time later, over the furious beat of his heart, I hear him say, "We will find out what happened to Kaylee, but we need to make sure you are safe first."

When I lift my eyes to his, wanting him to see my gratitude firsthand, the pleading in his eyes steals the air from my lungs. They're so beautiful, yet so painfully tormented, and I learn why when he mutters, "Please let me be a part of that."

"Maddox—"

"I would die without you, Demi. It would literally kill me." I'm on the verge of waterworks all over again when he whispers, "It *did* kill me."

I hate breaking his heart. I swore never to hurt him only minutes ago, but I've never been one to shy away from the massive elephant in the room. "Your family—"

"Will understand," Maddox interrupts, his reply resolute and to the point.

I breathe out my nerves before asking, "Are you sure this is what you want?"

"Yes," he replies without pause for thought. "Because I am right where I am meant to be. With you."

5

———————

MADDOX

My eyes drift to the bathroom door when the toilet flushes. Demi and I have been hiding out in Demi's hospital room for the past four days, waiting for news on what Agent Brahn's next move will be. In all honesty, I'm apprehensive about his plans. Don't misunderstand what I'm saying. Getting Demi away from her uncle is best for all involved, but I'm incredibly cautious about trusting an agent so soon after being brutally burned by one.

Tobias has the credentials to back up his claims he isn't rogue. He is a highly accredited agent who speaks fondly of his daughter. The knowledge he values her life more than his own assures me the track he's steering us toward will be rocky but worthwhile.

I somehow need to remember that when guilt creeps into my veins.

My family has been blowing up my phone since I raced away from them on my motorbike. Aware it would be highly suspicious for my death to concur consecutively with Demi's saw local law enforcement officers encouraging my parents to file a missing person report in my name earlier today. My motorbike was last scanned a hundred miles from Ravenshoe near dense bushland, my final message to my family said that I needed time to clear my head, and my bank accounts have remained untouched since I 'supposedly' filled my motorbike's tank with gas four days ago.

Their messages request for me to give them the chance to help me through my grief. They reveal without a doubt that they believe Tobias's ruse that Demi is dead and that I made the right decision when I put Demi above them. She has no one. Her father died years ago, her mother hasn't been seen since his death, and the male members of her family think of her as an object instead of a person, but that isn't why I chose her.

I love her.

It's a different love than the one I have for my family. It felt like I couldn't breathe when I thought she was gone. My heart refused to beat. I was numb and emotionless. I would have preferred death than to remain living like that. My 'disappearance' will hurt my family, but they will lean on each other for support. It's what the Walshs do.

As Demi exits the bathroom, a message from Justine pops up on the screen of my phone.

JUSTINE:

I miss you. Your voice. Your laugh. Your annoyingness. Please call me.

I shake my head when Demi says, "I understand if you want to change your mind, Maddox. I won't hold it against you."

The angst highlighting her tone switches to a giggle when I snag her wrist and tug her toward me. She falls into my lap with a ghost-like smile on her beautiful face. The tears she shed earlier are no longer visible. She wasn't crying because she's devastated we are moments away from leaving this life behind. She shed happy tears, pleased by my suggestion that she dump Dr. Falgar's pill prescription into the bin next to her hospital bed.

Our baby was a surprise, but that doesn't mean he or she wasn't wanted. Proof I'm not the slightest bit scared to face it all over again exposes that.

"What's your wager?" I ask Demi while dragging my index finger down her nose like I watched her father do anytime he dropped her off at school. Even on her darkest days, it calms her like nothing else. "Will Nurse Sandy rock up before or after I kiss you?"

Demi smiles in a way that has me forgetting the pain my family is currently enduring. My focus is solely on her happiness. "I'm feeling lucky, so I'll wager a blowjob that she bursts through the doors within ten seconds of your mouth landing on mine."

As she drags her teeth over her lower lip like she's hopeful she'll lose, my cock twitches beneath her ass. We've done nothing more than kiss the past four days, but I'd be a liar if I said it wasn't enough. The past week and a half have taught us there's more to our relationship than a sexual attraction. We have what it takes to last. We just need the chance to showcase that.

"And you, Maddox?" Demi's husky voice adds to the girthy rod digging into her ass. The past four days have been tough on her. She's been poked and prodded, and her arm resembles a pin cushion, but it has exposed how strong she is. I hate that it took the death of our baby to expose her fighting spirit, but it doesn't make my appreciation of her newfound warrioress any less potent. I wasn't lying when I said her life matters. It matters to me, and it should matter to her too. "What's your wager?"

With the chips stacked in my favor, I get cocky. "That I'll win no matter how soon she arrives."

I brush my tongue against Demi's lips, adding to my roundabout claim that I can't lose when I'm with her before delving it into her mouth. My life changed instantly when I took the life of another man, but it hasn't been all bad. Demi hasn't once looked at me differently. If anything, her stares are more admiring. If I didn't know any better, I'd swear she loves the idea of being protected by me.

I breathe in the exhale Demi pushes out when I drag my tongue along the roof of her mouth. I love how she responds to me. I could be doing something as simple as tracing a figure-eight pattern on her back while staring at the ceiling, yet her body would react as if my head was in between her legs.

"Three... four... five." Demi's perfectly timed breaths turn rampant when she reaches seven without interruption.

"Eight... nine... t—" I'm unsure if she groans or moans when she reaches the 'T' in ten. Her grunts all sound about the same. I realize it's the former when a *tut-tut* breaks across the room.

When Nurse Sandy's scorn doesn't have us coming up for air, she adds a shoe tap into the mix. She's sympathetic for what Demi went through and never gives me hell for sharing Demi's bed every night, but she's extremely objective about us giving Demi's body time to heal.

I've told her numerous times I'd never do anything to Demi against her wishes, but Nurse Sandy is just as adamant that Demi would disregard her discomfort to ensure my every whim was answered.

"A woman who's been hurt by those she loves doesn't realize love is meant to be painless," Nurse Sandy quotes for the third time this week when Demi's scowl becomes hot enough to scald. "Up on the bed, Missy. I have vitals to take."

I angle my head to hide my smile when Demi does as commanded with a whiny moan. She can pretend all she likes that she loathes Nurse Sandy, but both Nurse Sandy and I know better. She's stern with Demi because she realizes it's best to leave the nurturing to me.

"How is your bleeding?" Nurse Sandy asks after checking Demi's pulse and taking her blood pressure.

"It's good," Demi replies sheepishly. "It's almost all gone."

"That *is* good." Nurse Sandy smiles, assuring Demi it's okay to admit she's healing. Our baby won't be forgotten when she stops bleeding. He or she will forever live in our hearts. "With your condition, this part of your recovery usually lasts longer than normal. However, you appear to be right on track."

She lowers the sheet on Demi's bed before nudging her head to the pillow, wordlessly requesting for Demi to lay down. When Demi is in position, she places the sheet just below Demi's panty line before raising her dress so it sits under her bra. I grind my back molars together when Demi hisses from the nurse pushing on her stomach. Demi is as strong as an ox, so for her to express pain, she is really feeling it.

"Tenderness is also normal." After prodding Demi's stomach for a couple more seconds, Nurse Sandy lowers her dress then helps Demi into a seated position. "Did any excessive product matter expel overnight?"

Demi looks mortified. She isn't the only one. This is the second time I've heard our baby referred to as a 'product.' Its repetitiveness doesn't make it any easier to swallow, though.

"No," Demi replies a short time later. "My bleeding has been light."

Nurse Sandy taps the tip of her pen on Demi's file. "Good. That means Dr. Falgar got it all."

Although a combination of grief and guilt could be responsible for my emotional response, the 'it' part of her statement grates my last nerve, but before I can announce that, Demi takes up my campaign. "*It*? He or she wasn't an 'it.' That was a baby. *Our* baby." She gestures her hand to me during the 'our' part of her comment.

Remorse fills Nurse Sandy's eyes a mere second before a blubbering response leaves her mouth, "I'm very sorry. You are right. That was your baby. I will learn to word my responses better from here on out." Her cheeks turn a hue of pink as she grimaces. "It may take a little getting used to. It's rare for anyone around these parts to be upset about their loss." Her last two sentences are so soft, I'm confident they weren't meant to be heard by neither Demi nor me. "I'll be back in around an hour to draw some blood."

She looks like she wants to say more. Her lips twitch, but not a word seeps from her mouth. Demi waits for her to burst through her hospital room door before she shifts her eyes to me. They're full of sorrow.

"Don't you dare apologize." I've studied her enough the past eight weeks to know what she's thinking, so I won't mention the prior fifteen years. She's remorseful for snapping at Nurse Sandy. "If you hadn't said something, I would have." A ghost of a smile cracks her lips when I add, "I doubt my response would have been as polite as yours. You're so strong, Demi. So fucking determined. With time, you could run this entire state."

When a snicker creeps across the room, my neck cranks to the door of Demi's room so fast, my muscles scream in protest. I've heard that snarky, condescending gripe before. It came from the man who swore an oath to protect the integrity of his country, the same man who encouraged me to run drugs for a mobster so he could line his pockets with money. It came from the very man who switched me from an everyday American to a murderer. It came from Agent Arrow Moses.

"What the fuck are you doing here?" I leap from my chair, tug Demi off the bed, then pull her behind me. I wasn't lying when I said the best protection a woman can have is the ability to protect herself, but that's null and void when it comes to men like Agent Moses. "You're on leave without pay, awaiting prosecution. Your days at the Bureau are numbered."

I'm not saying anything I can to get Demi out of a dangerous situation. I'm speaking facts. Over two days, sixty men dug through a mountain load of rubbish searching for the wire Agent Moses bugged me with that fateful night weeks ago. I thought Agent Brahn was wasting time we didn't have on matters no longer significant, but he proved otherwise when his crew achieved the seemingly impossible. They found both the device and the teeny tiny thumb print Agent Moses left inside the tape compartment of the recorder.

Even without knowing the full extent of Agent Moses's crimes, Agent Brahn was confident he had enough evidence to take the matter further. He immediately put actions in place to have Agent Moses stood down. I have no shame admitting I smirked like a smug prick when I heard he had been placed on an unpaid suspension pending further investigations.

"Whatever do you mean, Ox?" Agent Moses asks, drawing my focus back to him. "I took a couple days of leave to fatten up my dossier. Promotions are rare at the Bureau. You should never apply for one until *all* your i's are dotted and your t's are crossed." He moseys into the room like he owns the place. "Didn't Tobias tell you that? From what I've heard, you've had plenty of time for snitching the past four days." He holds his index finger in the air when I attempt to interrupt him. "Oh, that's right. I forgot about the 'special' assignment Agent Brahn had to attend." He air quotes 'special' like the arrogant prick he is. "I bet he wishes he weren't so eager now." When confusion crosses my face, lost as to why he's smiling like he has the world at his feet, he asks, "Did you not read the papers I had specially delivered?"

When he nudges his head to a stack of newspapers on the wheelie table at the end of Demi's bed, Demi advises, "The tea lady delivered them when you were in the shower. I assumed you had ordered them."

Her hot breath fans the sweat beading on my neck when I shake my head. I've been struggling to ignore the pleas my family bombarded my phone with the past four days. I didn't need to read about their grief.

It's the fight of my life not to rearrange Agent Moses's face with my fists when he says with a chuckle, "You really should keep up with the news. It's amazing what you can learn within a couple of sentences."

Even with my brain screaming for me not to fall for his tricks, I snatch up the first newspaper in the stack, then drag my eyes over the print. It takes barely a second to discover the reason for Agent Moses's cockiness. His role at the Bureau hasn't just been reinstated, he is now also the acting supervisor for this state's division of the FBI.

What. The. Fuck?

"How? Why?" Entire sentences are above me right now. "Agent Brahn would *never* allow this to happen."

I choke on my spit when Agent Moses informs without remorse, "Tobias is dead."

I want to call him a liar. I want to tell him I'll never fall for his tricks again, but there's too much honesty in his eyes to discount. He's telling the truth, and the smallest article under the news of his appointment backs up his claims.

Agent Tobias Brahn was killed on duty.

His funeral is later this week.

I am the first to admit I'm not good at thinking on the spot, and it's showcased in the worst way when the floating of the newspaper to the floor is quickly chased by me smashing my fist into Agent Moses's nose.

He's so unprepared for my hit, he sails back with waving arms and a mangled groan. When he collides with the door of Demi's room, his head's collision with the super thick wood is the loudest part of his fall. He's dazed in an instant, and even quicker than that, I rip Demi's medical chart off the end of her bed, then demand her to put on a coat.

"Hurry," I instruct before moving toward the corridor to

check the coast is clear. Agent Moses is starting to rouse, and his groggy awakening has me eager for more than one hit. I can't do that and get Demi out of the danger zone at the same time.

She must come first.

Once Demi has her jacket in place and her shoes on, I prop a dazed Agent Moses onto the wall across from the door. He murmurs something about me choosing my battles, but since blood is gushing out of his nose, and his head is all types of woozy, I can't understand a thing he says.

It's for the best. I'm so close to killing him, he should count his lucky stars that I don't want Demi witnessing me taking another man's life. If she weren't standing beside me, all bets would be off. That's how much I despise Agent Moses.

"There are cameras at the end of the hall. Keep your head down and your hair in front of your face." I tug out the elastic that forever keeps Demi's hair in place before pushing down on the door handle. I don't know where we'll go once we leave here, I barely have funds for a cab fare since I left my gym bag in the cab four days ago. I just know I need to get her as far from here as possible. If Agent Moses is aware she is alive, it will be only a matter of time before her uncle also finds out.

I freeze halfway out the door when Demi says my name in a breathless plea. When I whip around to face her, she balances onto her tippy toes, then plants her lips on mine. Her kiss isn't a long embrace, nor is it sloppy with a heap of tongue. It's a perfect kiss full of love and mutual respect. A kiss that exposes I could have killed Agent Moses, and she wouldn't have looked at me differently. A kiss so passionate, I'd give anything to go back in time to when she mashed her face into my crotch in Saint's ride. Her life was far from perfect back then, but it was a heap less dangerous than it is now.

"I love you," Demi whispers over my mouth before she bobs under my arm to move into the corridor.

Once she has her chin balancing on her chest, she commences walking down the eerily quiet space that's usually a bustling hive of activity.

I take a moment to acknowledge the warning gurgle of my stomach before shadowing Demi's walk.

We make it to the foyer, where the elevator banks are located before our departure is noticed. Mercifully, it isn't an armed guard with tattooed guns and a nasty sneer. It's Nurse Sandy. "*Go,*" she mouths after straying her eyes away from the direction we just sprinted.

I can't see what she can see, but if the terror on her face is anything to go by, she's spotted Agent Moses's bloody nose and rapidly darkening eyes.

The crash of a medical trolley colliding into someone's thigh sounds through my ears at the same time the elevator doors snap shut with Demi and me inside. I doubt Nurse Sandy's interference will slow Agent Moses's pursuit by much, but I am grateful she put both herself and her position on the line for us.

With my focus more on the stairwell at the side of the elevator than the foyer of the hospital, I don't realize we're sprinting straight toward disaster until our burst through the rotating hospital doors has me crashing into one of Col's goons. It isn't the man who shoved his gun into Demi's ribs weeks ago. It's the one who was sitting in the driver's seat, smirking like a smug fuck in the rearview mirror when Col forced Demi's goodbye kiss to land on his mouth instead of his cheek.

"So it is true," mutters a familiar voice at our right. "The dead do resurrect."

When Col slides out of the backseat of his Audi, I fist up, ready and willing to go down fighting. I only need to keep him and his goon occupied long enough for Demi to flee like her father did when she was seven. I'm more than capable of doing that. In a sick way, I'm looking forward to it.

Col smirks. "That won't be necessary. Not even *she* will permit you to throw a punch when she discovers what I have up my sleeve." He doesn't need to say Demi's name for me to know who he's referencing. The sneer the 'she' part of his threat was delivered with is indicative enough.

"No!" Demi squeals when she spots a blonde in the back seat of Col's town car. Sloane is busted up, crying, and bound. The clothes she's wearing are designer, but they've been put through the wringer, even homeless people would turn their noses up at them.

Demi whacks into me as fiercely as Sloane did Saint weeks ago when I curl my arm around her waist and hoist her away from Sloane before she can get within an inch of her. She calls me names and warns that she'll never forgive me if I don't let her go.

She beats into me so viciously, she misses Col advising me that I know where to find him if I want Sloane to finish her studies. "It'll do you best to show up. Trust me when I say there's no place for hate in a relationship." Confident I'll fall into step before I'd ever disappoint Demi, Col clicks his fingers together two times before he slides back into his Audi, pushing Sloane across the blood-stained leather seat in the process. "Nine o'clock, Ox. Not a second later."

He doesn't need to tell me what will happen to Sloane if I don't show up. She will be dead, and Demi will hate me for eternity. She doesn't directly say that while fighting to get away from me, but the painful sob she releases when her uncle's Audi glides down the hill of Mercer Private most certainly reflects that.

Furthermore, she's already grieving our child. She won't survive back-to-back losses.

"No," Demi cries on a sob when Col's car disappears from view, all but convinced her best friend is dead. "I was supposed to keep her safe. She wasn't meant to get hurt."

"It will be okay. I promise I won't let anything happen to her."

After locking our eyes, I hit her with the same pleading, despondent look I gave her on the freeway weeks ago. It impacts her more than my words ever could. Her eyes are wide and terrified, but she immediately stops thrashing against me, her energy reserved to free the worry I still see in her eyes. "You can't fight for him, Maddox. It will destroy you."

I brush off her claims with a halfhearted shrug. I'm not a killer. Just the thought of ending another man's life rushes memories of Igor's last breath to the forefront of my mind, but I can do it for Demi. She comes before anyone—even me.

Furthermore, murder is already notched on my ledger. Saint's is still clean. I don't see that being the case if he discovers the real reason for Sloane's absence the past couple of days.

While rubbing my thumb over the vein pulsating in Demi's wrist, I press my lips to the shell of her ear. "I can do this, Demi. I can do it for you."

When she fails to fire an objection, I place her back onto her feet. She pivots around to face me so fast, her hair slaps her face. Demi's cheeks are white, and tears are damming in her eyes, but once again, her focus isn't on herself. It isn't even on me. All her attention is rapt on one man. Agent Moses. He is watching our interaction like this was the exact response he was aiming for. His my-shit-doesn't-stink smirk all but confirms my earlier theories that he has teamed up with the very men he's meant to be hunting.

Demi doesn't fight me when I impede her steps for the second time today. It could be because Agent Moses's swollen eye makes her urge to punish him less vital or the words I whisper in her ear. I'm truly unsure. "It's in our best interest for him to believe I'm going to fight tonight."

As I guide her to a taxi rank a couple of spots up, her confused eyes bounce between mine. She doesn't want me to fight, but she's convinced we don't have any other option. I believed the same thing only moments ago. Regretfully for Agent Moses, his lack of dignity reminded me of a famous quote my father shared when I was a child. *"If you fight for what you believe in, you may lose, but if you don't fight at all, you've already lost."*

I don't have the means to fight men like Col and Agent Moses and come out of the wreckage uninjured, but I know someone who could. I simply need to convince him that royal lineage means nothing when the hierarchy of the realm neglects the dignitaries stabilizing his foundations, and the perfect person to help him see sense through the madness lives only a stone's throw away.

MADDOX

"You're fuckin' crazy if you think I'll go through with this." Rocco points to Demi milling in the lobby of his palatial home. She's unsure why I brought her here, but she is so blinded by worry, she's following my plan after asking only a handful of questions. "Your girl ain't dead, Ox. How about you take that as a win."

"But her friend—"

"Isn't my problem," he interrupts, his voice a roar that startles Demi even from a distance. She's been extra jittery since we left Mercer Private. She is barely gripping reality. One push in the wrong direction could completely overwhelm her. I must tread carefully, but I also must do it quickly. Time is not in our favor.

"So you're going to let a girl be raped and mutilated by a group of men and do *nothing* about it." As far as I am aware, Sloane and Rocco have never crossed paths, but that doesn't mean I can't use Rocco's hate of rapists against him. His response to his mother and sister being abused is a clear sign he loathes woman-beaters, and I'm desperate enough to use the knowledge against him. "Col was going to auction Demi off. There were no stipulations to her sale. They could do whatever they pleased to her. Cut her. Rape her. Torture her. Nothing was off-limits!"

"All right, fuck face. I get the point." Rocco works his jaw side to side before adding, "But the girl you want to help isn't Demi, which means she ain't my problem." I don't announce I can hear a 'but' hanging in the air. He doesn't give me the chance. "But that doesn't mean I can't fiddle around with some things. See if I can get the ball rolling in your favor."

"We need more than a ball, Rocco. This isn't a fucking tennis match." The clenching of his fists warns me to tread carefully, but forever stubborn, I rip off the Band-Aid with one fell swoop. "Dimitri needs to be involved. He is the *only* one capable of going against Col and living to tell the tale."

Rocco rubs his hands together like he relishes the idea of hearing Col take his last breath, but he also shakes his head. "Dimi ain't got time for this."

"He would if he thinks it concerns his daughter, Fien."

Before I can blink, Rocco pins me to the wall of his living room by my throat. "How *the fuck* do you know Fien is his daughter?" he screams in my face, coating my cheek with his spit.

"He told me about h—"

"Bullshit," he interrupts, cutting me off. "Dimi doesn't share *anything* about his family with *anyone*. Not even his family, so you either quit lying, or I'll remove digits until you learn without a doubt how much I hate liars."

If it were any other day but today, the truthfulness in his tone would have me shitting bricks. Sadly, I don't feel fear when protecting the people I love. "Dimitri told me about Fien when I confronted him about using my sister as bait."

The tenseness in Rocco's jaw doubles, but since nothing but honesty is heard in my reply, he has no choice but to believe me. "So you're the reason I've been on his shitlist the past week?"

Some may call me an idiot for nodding, but I'll wear the title with honor if it gets Rocco on board with my plan. I don't need Dimitri to fight my battles. I need him to understand the storm his father is raining down on his cousin.

"Dimitri showed me Fien's photo, said she comes before anyone."

"She *does* come before anyone," Rocco clarifies, walking straight into my trap.

"Then shouldn't he want to end the violence that occurs to women in his industry to ensure she's adequately protected? Fien is mafia royalty." When Rocco nods, agreeing with me, I hook my thumb in the direction Demi is standing. "So the fuck is Demi, but that hasn't stopped her uncle, *the king of your realm,* from threatening to sodomize her. She's his fucking niece. His blood. Yet, he still wants to treat her like a whore." With how hot my blood is, I'm shocked I can talk, much less in a cool, calm, and collected manner. "I get it. All right. I understand. Everyone has a place in this realm. I just hope like hell Col changes his sick ways before Fien shows up, or who knows what will happen to her."

I have him now—hook, line, and fucking sinker. He wants to castrate Col. He wants to hang him via his intestines. But regretfully, he's also aware not even someone as high up as him can do that. Dimitri can't even end his father's reign. Col can only be taken out two ways. He either hands the reins to his son or castrates himself. Since the latter will never happen, Dimitri must force him to do the former. Discovering he is liaising with the wrong side of the law could be the beginning of that. I just need Rocco to convince him there's a good reason for him to interfere in his father's business adventures. His daughter could be the missing puzzle piece I'm seeking.

After a couple of seconds of deliberation, Rocco says, "If this goes sour—"

"I fully expect you to throw me under the bus."

The relief I've finally gotten through to him shifts to anger when he mutters, "And take up residency with your girl." He pats my shirt like the heat roaring through his body will iron out the crinkles he caused before he moves for a pack of cigarettes on the coffee table. "I've seen the way she looks at me. She's totally into me."

I want to tell him he doesn't stand a chance with Demi, but since it will ruin the second half of my plan, I continue our negotiation as if he isn't attempting to start a pissing contest. "Talking about Demi… I need another favor." The firmness of Rocco's jaw exposes that I've outstayed my welcome, but his failure to verbally announce that also gives me the silent go-ahead. "I need a place for her to bunker down for a couple of hours. Somewhere she'll be safe."

Rocco lights the cigarette dangling between his quirked lips before asking, "You want her to stay here?" When I jerk up my chin, he shakes his head. "No can do. The only women who make it past the foyer of my home are here to be thoroughly fucked. You don't want that to happen, Ox, because she'll be all like 'did you put it in yet?' by the time I'm done with her."

"She's your best friend's cousin."

"And?" he asks, acting ignorant to the fury in my tone. "Do you think that'll stop me? Certainly didn't work with his sister." Smoke puffs out of his nose when he realizes his error. This is the second time he's referenced Ophelia while spilling secrets this week. I don't see Dimitri taking kindly to either of his confessions, but since I'm desperate for him to believe we're on the same team, I'm not going to mention that.

When he realizes I'm not going to use his slip-up against him, Rocco stabs out his scarcely touched cigarette before taking a seat in one of the royal-looking chairs nestled around his living room. "Your girl can't stay here because if there's no one to subdue Dimitri's anger when he realizes we played him, we'll be wearing concrete boots by the morning."

I twist my lips, a little lost. "What do you mean?"

Rocco points to Demi. "She isn't Fien, but Dimi can't look at her without imagining if his daughter will turn out like her. The Petretti genes are strong. There's no denying them." He stands to his feet like he's bored with our conversation before he jerks his head to the stairwell on our left. "The guest bedroom is stacked with everything you'll need. Wash up and get ready for your night, treat your girl like the princess she is, then head out, taking her with you. I'll do what I can, Ox, but I make no promises."

His words offer no guarantee, but the briefest glance he directs at Demi while bypassing her in the foyer most certainly does. He hates that we've put him in this situation, but he'd rather swim in shit than see Demi hurt.

"What did he say?" Demi asks once the healthy rumble of an engine fades to a barely audible buzz.

"He's going to try."

"Try?" Demi parrots, her tone low. She was hoping for more than a half-assed pledge.

Rocco can't give that to her, but I most certainly can.

"What he can't do, I can."

She reads me as no one else can. "I don't want you to fight, Maddox. I just want…"

"Sloane safe and well?" I fill in when words elude her.

She peers at me with her big, beautiful eyes out in full force before bobbing her head.

"Then we'll do that. Together. Me and you, all right?" I track my finger across the faintest silver sliver in her cheek while muttering, "We can't let the bullies win. If we do…"

"We're just as big of a bully," we say at the same time, smiling as the memory of my mom saying that very thing to us in the second grade fills our heads.

With my mood not as hostile as it was moments ago, I take Rocco up on his offer of a shower. I'm not dirty—it's hard to work up a sweat in a twelve-foot by twelve-foot room when sexual activities are off the agenda—but I do feel a little grubby. This industry has a way of making you dirty even when you're not.

If I were honest, I'd also admit I want to pamper Demi like she deserves. I haven't trained in over a week, and with Col most likely still pissed about my win last month, he'll summon his biggest, baddest fighter for tonight's match.

I refuse to walk into the arena blind like I did last time. I put my life in the hands of law enforcement and scarcely walked away with my dignity intact. Who knows who the odds will favor this time around? Dimitri isn't his father, but you can't be raised by a monster and not have some of his grubbiness rub off on you. If my plan fails, this afternoon could be my final hours with Demi. I'm not giving them up for anyone.

Don't misread what I'm saying. I'll *never* do anything to Demi she isn't up for. I just want to hold her a little. Cherish her how she deserves to be cherished. I also want to love her like she's never been loved.

When a monstrous bed in the room at the front of the top floor announces it is most likely the master suite, I guide Demi down the hall in the opposite direction. Halfway down, I spot a room that represents the one Rocco mentioned. The king-size bed has fresh towels stacked on it, the closet is brimming with clothes for all genders, and the attached bathroom is as big as the room. It's the perfect spot to show Demi not all men are pricks.

Understanding of Nurse Sandy's saying pummels into me when our entrance into the room is quickly followed by Demi shrugging off her jacket. She's panicked out of her mind for her friend, but not even a bucketload of guilt allows her to say no to me. She still doesn't realize love is meant to be painless.

"Huh," Demi mutters in confusion when I snag a towel off the mattress before leading her into the bathroom. I can't lie. The disappointment fueling her groan swells my chest. She can't deny me, but part of that is because she doesn't want to deny me.

Want and can't are two very different things.

"Let me," I request when Demi commences unbuttoning the buttons on her dress.

I switched on the faucet.

She knows where I'm going with this.

While staring into her eyes, I undo the top four buttons on her dress before pulling it over her head. A ghost-like grin curves my lips when she can't hold back her smile at my caveman ways. The buttons in her dress go to the hem, so I could have removed it with ease if I had an ounce of patience. That is something I'll never have when it comes to Demi.

Demi's panted breaths fan my neck when I twist my arms around her back to undo her bra. She gasps softly when I have the three prongs undone in an impressive two seconds.

Once I've dumped her bra onto her dress, I lower my hands to the rim of her panties. "It's okay," I assure her when she curls her hand over mine, panicked I'm about to see a womanly product she's certain will offend me. "All you need to do is step out of them. I promise I won't look."

Lying has never been a strong point of mine, but I see it becoming easier if it lessens Demi's hesitation as quickly as it does this time around. Her teeth only graze her bottom lip for the slightest bit before she presses her palms to my shoulders, then steps out of the cotton material I lowered to her ankles.

Wanting to show her she has nothing to be ashamed about, I remove the thankfully empty pad from her underwear, fold it together, toss it in the bin at the side of the vanity, then tug out the hair tie she put in during our commute to Rocco's place.

"How about we get you cleaned up? These products don't look as nasty as the ones at the hospital." Demi almost always wears her hair up and out the way, and the low-quality shampoo and conditioner supplied by Mercer Private gave her the perfect excuse. It knotted her hair more than it made it glossy and smooth.

Demi looks torn between sobbing and smiling when I step us into the shower. I guide her back until her long locks are drenched by the water pumping out of the showerhead. Her hair is so thick, it takes me running my fingers through the tangled waves to ensure they're fully wet.

There's no doubt which way her emotions swing when I crack open an untouched bottle of shampoo, squeeze a dollop of the fruity product into my palm, then commence massaging it into her scalp. Her eyes are full of turmoil, but she knows as well as I do that Col won't hurt Sloane more than he already has. Without her, he has no bargaining chip to wager with tonight. He won't give that up any more than I'll ever deny Demi this much-deserved moment of peace.

"Close your eyes," I say with a breathy chuckle, equally mortified and pleased she'd risk burning her eyes with shampoo so she wouldn't miss out on the opportunity of returning my yearning stare. "You'll get shampoo in your eyes if you keep gawking at me like you are."

"Totally worth it," she murmurs a mere second before she balances on her tippytoes to plant her lips on mine.

We kiss long enough there's no doubt all the suds in her hair are washed out, then we kiss some more once her hair is drowned in conditioner.

What? Even guys know you have to let the conditioner soak in. It makes its moisturizing powers more effective.

I run my index finger down Demi's nose when she groans about the withdrawal of my mouth a couple of seconds later. It won't keep her needs contained for long, but it does advise her I'm struggling as much as she is. Not touching her is the equivalent of torture for me. I'm just aware she needs this even more than I need my hands on her to breathe.

When the happy gleam in her eyes switches to sexual frustration, I say, "I brought you in here to get clean, not to mess you up."

Memories of the first time we fooled around in a bathroom roll through my head when Demi replies, "You can be clean and messy at the same time, and you don't even need to know how to multitask to do it." She swivels on the spot, her earlier anguish up and vanished. "Trust me. It's a lot of fun."

I send a voiceless warning to my cock to calm down when the grazing of her teeth over her lower lip this time around occurs without an ounce of guilt in her eyes. She's forgotten all about the shitstorm raining down on us. Once again, it's just her and me against the world—*exactly how it's meant to be.*

After a beat, I nudge my head to the tiled shelf housing the bottles of shampoo, conditioner, and body wash. "Put your foot on the bench, I can hear your thoughts. With how wickedly dirty they are, I'll need to scrub your skin raw." Not an ounce of malice is heard in my tone. I'm as lost in the chemistry brewing between us as Demi.

When Demi does as asked, I squeeze a generous dollop of strawberry-scented shower gel into the palm of my hand. There are untouched shower puffs on the tiled bench Demi is balancing her foot on, but I'd rather use my hand. Then I can feel the effect my touch has on her body as well as see it.

It's going to be a glorious couple of minutes.

Once my hands are loaded with bubbles, I place them on each side of Demi's right ankle before dragging them up her calf. Her legs are lean and smooth, meaning two hands is a little obsessive, but what can I say? I like having my hands on her that I'll always use two no matter how snug the area I'm nurturing.

Yes, you read that as intended.

The thrusts of Demi's chest double when I slide my hands past her knee and up her thigh before stopping at the base of her sex that smells more scrumptious than the body wash coating her skin. The scent of her pussy has me wanting to be a ravishing caveman. I'd give anything to demand her sweet pussy to my mouth so I could feast on it like a Viking, but I also know she needs a gentle, caring lover right now, not a savage beast who could eat her pussy for hours without coming up for air.

"Not yet," I push out with a moan after cleaning her pussy with three carefully placed scrubs. I don't plunge two fingers inside of her as my cock is demanding. I gently glide them through the folds of her pussy while staring at the throb in her throat so I can time her breaths. One wrong quiver, and I'll withdraw contact quicker than a bullet being fired from a gun.

After cleaning her left leg as effectively as I did her right, I shift my focus to Demi's midsection. Conscious of the pained groan she released when Nurse Sandy took her vitals, I'm extra cautious with her stomach. I don't want to cause her more pain. The emotional toll of a miscarriage is already confronting, not to mention almost losing your life in the process. My emotions are teetering, so I'd hate to think how Demi's are handling the complex situation.

I am devastated she lost our baby, but I am so fucking grateful I didn't lose her, I've placed the loss of our child to the back of my mind. He or she will be mourned. I just can't do that *and* ensure Demi's well-being isn't sitting in the grinder mine was minced in when I thought I had lost her.

The world wobbles beneath my feet when I raise my sudsy hands to Demi's breasts. Her fantastic tits could revamp the centerfold industry. They're not pompously large, but they are more than a handful, have perfect symmetry, and her light brown nipples always stand to attention, pleading to be fondled.

They peak even more when I glide my hands over them. With the bliss in her eyes shining brighter than worry, I give her breasts an extra scrub before raising my hands to her shoulders. Let me assure you, it's a fucking hard feat. One I'm doubtful I would have achieved if it weren't for the morals my parents raised me with.

My life changed in an instant when I took another man's life, but it will take staining my hands with more than one man's blood for years of teachings to be forgotten. Besides, I didn't kill Igor for fun. I did it to protect Demi. And I'd do it again if it produced the same results. The past couple of weeks have been tough, but my relationship with Demi is stronger. I truly believe we can survive anything.

By the time Demi's body is coated with suds, the amount of blood inflating my cock has me on the verge of coronary failure, and Demi looks close to climaxing. I didn't think this through. This is way harder than I thought it would be, and no, I'm not solely referencing my cock.

The struggle to keep things friendly is heard in my voice when I say, "Step under the spray so I can wash off the suds."

With her eyes locked on me, Demi does as requested without protest. The purposely-scalding water glides down her enticing chest, over the smooth planes of her stomach, past her fragrant-smelling pussy, and weaves around her legs before it circles the drain along with the suds of shower gel.

I watch their gurgle before raising my hands to Demi's hair to remove the conditioner from her thick locks. As her hair returns to its previously glossy appearance, I pray like fuck my moral compass doesn't follow the shower gel's descent to hell.

This is cocky for me to admit, but fuck it, I'm not ashamed. My dick is so hard, it stabs into Demi's stomach like it can burrow its way to her pussy via her belly button. It's that desperate to penetrate her, it is willing to take any hole on offer.

The humor my inner monologue hits me with chops up my words when I say, "There you go. All clean."

I angle my head to the side when Demi thwarts my attempt to shut off the shower faucet by stepping into the path. "If I want to be treated like a queen, I sure as hell need to consider you as my king."

My cock almost takes out her eye when she bends down to gather the shower gel from the in-built bench her foot was precariously balancing on moments ago. She could have reached it without bending her knees, but she's a tease and more than happy for me to know it.

After squeezing a large dollop onto her palm, she raises her eyes to mine, licks her lips, then proves no matter how much I try to subdue the sexual chemistry between us, it will never fully extinguish. She doesn't start her scrub of my body at my ankles. She commences it at my dick. And she doesn't just scrub it clean, she tugs it, strokes it, and massages the vein feeding it with the pad of her thumb.

"Demi… fuck. We can't." I'm telling her no, but the rock of my hips is on the other end of the spectrum. My body doesn't want to deny her any more than I don't want to disappoint her. "I want to take care of you."

I should be immediately shutting this down, pulling back, doing anything but encouraging Demi's defiance by rocking my monster dick in and out of her circled hand, but my response can't be helped. The shower gel replicates the silky softness of her mouth when she gives me the best head I've ever been given, and her unclipped nails replicate the grazes her teeth make when she drags them over the crown of my cock.

"You *are* taking care of me," Demi counterbids, her words as smooth and precise as the strokes she does to my cock. "And I am taking care of you." She lifts her eyes to mine. They're beautiful and free and oh-so-wickedly deviant. "I just happen to love you *and* your cock equally, so I'm killing two birds with one stone. It's what makes me a great multitasker."

Fuck morals. Her smile has me convinced repenting my sins for eternity will be easier than giving this up.

"At the first sign of trouble, I'm out."

Demi grins victoriously. "I wouldn't expect any less."

After pressing a kiss to the middle of my chest, she lowers her eyes to my cock, eager to watch it sliding in and out of her hand. Within a couple of strokes, the muscles in my thighs tense before my hips begin to gyrate in rhythm to her strokes. It feels so fucking good, and we're not hurting anyone, so I throw back my head and get caught up in the sensation, lessening the amount of weight I'm carrying on my shoulders.

It is amazing how liberating something as simple as being given a hand job in the shower can make me feel. My stomach has been a twisted ball of nerves all week, but right now, I feel like I could walk into a lion's den and walk out without a scratch. That's how freeing Demi's touch is to me. She makes me feel invincible.

"Fuck yes, just like that."

After increasing the pressure of her thumb on the vein running down my shaft, Demi adds a sexy twist to her pumps. Every inch of my cock is covered, and just when I think it couldn't possibly feel any better, she finds my lips in the steamy conditions and nibbles on them like she usually does my balls.

While groaning through the sensation gripping every inch of my sack, I plant my hands against the tiles on either side of Demi's head before bending my knees. Not only can I now grind my cock in and out of her hand as if it is her pussy, but she can also reach my mouth without overstretching her spine.

I wouldn't necessarily say we kiss as she pumps my cock for its seed. We more grunt into each other's mouth, pant, and share the minute bit of air that hasn't been gobbled up by the electricity brewing between us.

"In case you're wondering, even now, on the cusp of blowing my load all over your stomach and fantastic tits, I'm still thinking about how sugary your pussy tastes." I lick her lips before plunging my tongue inside her mouth, hopeful as fuck the warm welcome it always receives will stop me from falling to my knees and confirming her pussy tastes as sweet as I'm recalling.

As Demi duels her tongue with mine, she strokes me faster. Harder. Oh-so-fucking perfectly. I never knew a hand job could feel so good. I stroked my cock over her for years. Not once did it feel this good. Demi has a way of making the most mundane tasks seem as if they are unachievable by the average man.

"I'm fucking close," I mutter a couple of seconds later, my wish to come heard in my tone.

"I know," Demi murmurs over my mouth as she pants and grunts. "So am I."

The knowledge she's close to orgasming by doing something as simple as stroking my dick has cum racing from my balls to the crest of my cock. Its sprint is too furious for me to contain. I come with a hoarse moan while chanting Demi's name on repeat.

As hot spurts of cum hit her chest, Demi grips my cock tighter, her pursuit relentless even with her pushing me to the pinnacle of perfection. She works my dick so well, the veins in my shaft soon throb as if it didn't seek release only moments ago. While matching her strokes grind for grind, I lower my eyes to the murky white streams of cum extending from the generous curves of her breasts to the sexy dip in the lower half of her stomach.

Caught up in the moment, I gather a large splat of cum from her breast, then lower my hand to the apex of her thighs. When I rub the still-warm byproduct of my climax into Demi's clit with my thumb, she fans open her shuddering thighs, welcoming my touch. I suck in the moan she pushes out when I slip two fingers inside of her. Her promise that she was on the brink of climax is proven honest when my fingers find the sweet spot inside of her. It usually takes a couple of strokes of her G-spot to set her off. Today, it only takes one gentle rub.

After burrowing her head between my pecs, Demi massages my fingers with her vaginal walls. She chants, moans, and comes undone while grinding her clit against the palm of my hand. The pure bliss of her face when she climaxes thickens my cock to the point it is painful. I'm hard in an instant, and it takes everything I have not to curl Demi's legs around my waist and drive home.

I doubt I would have held back if the removal of my fingers from Demi's snug pussy didn't occur with a heap of redness. She's bleeding, and once again, it's my fault.

"It's okay," I assure Demi when the idyllic look on her face is gobbled up with horror. I'm dying a little on the inside knowing I hurt her, but I'll never let her know that. "It's nothing that can't be cleaned up with a bit of water."

I shove my hand under the spray, gulping when Demi's blood rolls down my fingers before it circles the drain. Logically, I know that isn't our baby, but there's a fucked-up part in my brain that hasn't worked that out just yet.

Proof Demi knows me better than anyone is undeniable when she whispers, "That isn't our baby."

"I know." I raise my eyes from the drain to Demi. "Still hurts a little, though. It's not our baby, but it is there because we lost our baby."

Sadness fills Demi's eyes with tears, but they're scarcely seen through her pride. The past four days taught us that communication needs to be one of our strongest points. We can have an abundance of sexual chemistry and a mutual attraction fiery enough to start a blaze, but we'll never make it out of this fucked-up realm unscarred if we don't start expressing ourselves with more than touch. We've been doing that the past four days, and we will continue doing that until we take our final breaths.

After ensuring the blood on Demi's thighs is cleared away, I turn off the faucet, then step out of the shower to fetch the towel. "Is it crazy for me to admit I was excited about the prospect of becoming a dad?"

It takes everything Demi has not to let the dam in her eyes spill over when she shakes her head, but she does it. She proves she's stronger than even I could have predicted. "I would have been more shocked if you had reacted negatively." She steps closer to me with nurturing, sorrow-filled eyes. "That's why I should have been honest with you from the start."

It takes me a couple of seconds to realize what she's saying, but when I unearth the reason behind her remorse, I'm nearly knocked on my ass. "You knew you were pregnant?"

"Not officially." She scoops my hand in hers like she's afraid I might bolt. "I had an inkling when Rocco pointed out some observations during your last fight. He was the one who brought me the tests."

I had wondered how she had gotten them. Now everything makes sense—including Rocco's protectiveness of her the morning we got into a tussle. He didn't threaten to throw Demi to the wolves when I pushed him for a fairer compromise. Only my ass was on the line.

"Landon's words were in my head when I ripped open the first test. I truly didn't know which way I wanted the results to go." A faint grin curls Demi's lips as her eyelids flicker in memory. "I think I broke the Walsh family record." Her ghost-like smirk turns into a full-blown smile. "It didn't even take me a second to fall in love."

I run my index finger down her nose, needing to touch her but so desperate not to hurt her to keep things simple. "Is that why you took the other two tests? To stretch out the timeline?"

She waits for me to wrap her in the towel before she shakes her head, her nose crinkling. "They were to back up my claims I wasn't crazy for lying on our bed for the next hour with my hands curled over my stomach."

I grin at the thought of her being in complete awe in under thirty seconds. It was the same for me when she peered up at me for the first time in the second grade. I was a fucking goner, and every member of my family knew it.

The high curve of my lips shifts downward when Demi faintly adds, "Then it all came tumbling down within an hour of me taking a prenatal vitamin."

I follow her somber walk into the main part of the room while asking, "What vitamin did you take again?"

We've had similar discussions to this the past couple of days, but since we were in a hospital room and she had been poked and prodded, I never broadened my inquiries. There's a time and a place for everything. The hospital that saved Demi's life by ending our child's wasn't the place. I'm not sure now is the right time either, but what can I say? Curiosity killed the cat, but satisfaction brought it back.

Demi shrugs. "It was a generic pharmacy brand."

"That had your name printed on the label?" I ask after recalling parts of our previous conversation.

She stops halfway across the room before spinning around

to face me. She looks worried, but not even a threat of harm would stop her from lifting her chin. "Is that not normal?"

Truly unsure, my shoulder touches my ear when I do a one-shoulder shrug. I've never needed a prescription for the vitamins and protein supplements my trainer requested I took when I commenced my boxing career, but that doesn't necessarily mean everyone can buy them over the counter.

After taking a moment to gauge the response on my face, Demi snaps down to pick up her jacket from the floor. "Because it was in the packet Rocco left on the porch, I didn't put much thought into it appearing more like a prescription than an over-the-counter product. But it did say it was a multi-vitamin. I even searched the net to make sure I could take it in the first trimester. It said it was safe. I wouldn't have taken it if I believed otherwise."

"I don't doubt that." I step closer to her, hating that she thinks I'd ever believe she would put our baby in danger. "I'm just seeking answers. You previously said that you started cramping within an hour of taking the vitamin."

"I did," she agrees with a nod before removing one of the sanitary pads and a pair of panties she shoved into the pocket of her jacket before our sprint out of her hospital room. "The bleeding wasn't immediate..." Her brows furrow as she works through the fog still clouding her memories from that day. From our conversations the past four days, I've come to the conclusion that her miscarriage commenced with intense cramping. That's why she was in the shower, seeking relief from the pain with hot water. The steam from the endless hot water had her missing the soap that slipped from her grasp during a painful contraction-like cramp. She slipped and fell backward, hitting her head on the shower faucet. Although the impact didn't crack her skull, it was significant enough for her to sit dazed and confused in the shower for several long minutes. The amount of blood she lost was what kept her there for hours. "But the cramps were." As her eyes bounce between mine, salty blobs of wetness saturate them. "Do you think the vitamins I took had something to do with my miscarriage?"

I shake my head, even with the gurgle of my stomach portraying a completely different answer. A million scenarios have run through my head since I found her bleeding and unconscious in the cabin, but not once did this scenario cross my mind.

I didn't see the canister of vitamins during my second rummage through the cabin. That could have been because my mind was corrupted with grief, but that doesn't explain why the vitamins weren't on the shelf above the vanity sink where I saw them a mere second before stumbling onto Demi. Someone moved them, and it has me curious as to why they would do that.

Upon hearing the gurgles of my stomach, Demi secures the devotion of my eyes by curling her hand over my balled one. "I want someone to blame as well, Maddox. It's easier to blame than grieve, but Rocco would never be so cruel. He isn't like the other men in my uncle's industry. He has a heart."

The way I tugged on his heartstrings today to get him on our side adds proof to her claims Rocco isn't heartless like so many men in her family's 'business,' but there are two sides to Rocco. Two very different sides. "He's a killer, Demi. He can't be trusted."

"He is a killer. A *convicted* killer," she agrees without pause for thought. "But he can be trusted because if you truly believed otherwise, we wouldn't be here."

She has a point. I don't like it, but I can't deny it. I'm here because second only to me, Rocco will do everything in his power to keep Demi safe. I don't know where his protectiveness stems from or for how long it has been occurring, but I do trust that he'd never purposely lead Demi toward danger.

I wait for Demi to pull on a pair of panties she preloaded with a pad before saying, "I'd still like to look a little deeper into what you took. If that's all right with you?"

Her smile would have you convinced I asked her to marry me. "I'm fine with you doing that, and thank you for asking instead of telling me, but can it occur *after* we get Sloane back?" Her question has a double meaning. It not only implies she's hopeful her best friend will make it out of tonight's ordeal with only nightmares, but it also hints that she's convinced I'll be around after a second death-match to investigate the man I goaded into helping us.

Since I also refuse to consider the possibility our ruse may implode on us, I once again shift my focus from the shitstorm raining down on us, instead choosing to assert my efforts on the one thing I can do even while drowning on land.

Treating my girl like the princess she is.

"How much food do you think Rocco has in his fridge?"

Demi shrugs, unsure where I'm going with this but always willing to play with fire when it comes to me. "There's only one way to find out."

With a grin tugging her lips at one side, she tosses a pair of jeans from the overflowing closet into my chest, slips a cashmere long-sleeve dress over her head, then slides her hand into mine.

She leads our crusade through Rocco's house this time around. We're on the hunt for food, but if the current surging through the air is anything to go by, our night could end with more than a stomachache.

7

———

DEMI

The past six hours have been rough. Sloane hasn't left my thoughts for a second. I'm more than mindful it doesn't take much to split skin, but it is the scars not seen by the naked eye that I'm worried about the most. She knows nothing about my family—not a single thing—because I kept her sheltered from it. Was it stupid of me to do? Probably, but my uncle didn't give me much choice. If I paraded Sloane in front of him, I would have put her at risk.

Although I could have explained how dangerous he is, I would have struggled to do that in a legitimate way. If you're not born into this world, you would never believe how crazy it is without proof. Sloane's father adores her. He spoils her, promises her the world will be her oyster, and has her convinced women are equal in all corners of the globe.

In my uncle's industry that's far from the truth.

Well, it was until Maddox arrived on the scene.

He is the sole reason the past six hours have been so tiring.

My best friend—*my only friend*—is at the mercy of my ruthless uncle. Rules state she won't be hurt if Maddox arrives at the stipulated time tonight, which meant I was forced to pick between two horrifying choices. I either let my boyfriend face a murderer in the ring for the second time with the hope he would make it out of the carnage with only additional nightmares or leave Sloane defenseless.

The latter would alter who I am in an instant, making me not only unworthy of love but also incapable of expressing it. You can't claim to love someone, then leave them right when they need you the most. It isn't possible. That's why I'm clutching Maddox's hand for dear life, praying my instincts haven't led me astray today. Maddox wants me to have faith in his plan, and my job as his girlfriend is to do that. I trust him with my life, so it's only fair I also trust him with Sloane's as well.

"I need you to promise me something, Demi," Maddox murmurs from the driver's seat of our borrowed ride. "And no matter what happens, I need you to swear you'll follow through with your pledge."

My lips quiver when I reply, "You're scaring me." Not as much as the panic in his eyes, but it's there, nonetheless. "But I promise. Whatever it is, I'll do it."

Maddox's exhale ruffles my hair when it bounces off the windshield. "If I go down..." I try to interrupt him, but he squeezes my hand, denying me the opportunity. "*If* I lose... I need you to run."

To the boxing ring to help him?

To the authorities to call in for backup?

I can do either of those things, but if he's asking what I think he's asking, I *cannot* do that. I can't leave him when he needs me the most. I'd never forgive myself. The guilt would have me walking straight off a cliff like my father did.

I never understood why he left the way he did until my memories of Kaylee resurfaced. I'm struggling over the loss of a child I never met. My father's pain must have been unbearable. He just put on a brave front because he didn't know any different. Men are groomed to be emotionless in general, so you can only imagine how bad it is for the ones trapped in my uncle's realm.

My focus shifts back to the present when Maddox begs, "I need you to promise me, Demi. If I don't have a guarantee you will be safe no matter what, none of this will mean diddlysquat." He doesn't just mean our relationship, he means his life as a whole. That's how detrimental my safety is to him. He places it above his own life.

"You will win," I mumble through a sniffle. "I refuse to consider any other option."

He lowers his pressure on the gas pedal before straying his eyes to mine. "That's where the second half of my negotiation comes in." He licks his lips, hopeful a bit of moisture will help deliver his next sentence. "I don't want you scared of me—"

"I will *never* be scared of you."

He continues talking as if I never interrupted him. "I can't guarantee that will be the case if you witness me kill a man." Although I appreciate he's at least considering the possibility he will win tonight, I'm barely given a chance to relish it. "So, I'm asking for you to stay in the car."

"No," I answer with a brisk shake of my head. "Rocco said you need me there."

"*If* Dimitri shows up." Maddox's tone advises he thinks the odds of that occurring are extremely low. I can't blame his lack of optimism. Despite us bombarding his cell phone the past hour, we haven't heard from Rocco since he left his mega-mansion earlier today. "The parking lot is the prime location for you to spot his arrival. *If* he shows up, then you can come in, but only then, Demi. Not a moment before."

"No," I repeat, my head still shaking.

He squeezes my hand again, hating the disappointment in my tone but too determined to acknowledge it. "You promised."

"That was before I knew what you were asking. You are fighting for *me*. You're putting your life on the line for *me*. But you're denying *me* the opportunity to support you through this. *I* helped you find Igor's weak spot. *I* coached you through his crushing—"

"And *I* snapped his neck, Demi. Me." He bangs his chest with the hand that should be on the steering wheel. "*I* did that."

I hate that we're fighting, but I can't back down. "For *me*, Maddox. You did that for *me*." I drag the back of my hand under my nose to ensure nothing gross is spilling before sliding across the bench seat so that I am close enough to him for him to see the honesty in my eyes when I pledge, "I promise to run to another country *if* you lose. I promise to stare at my feet long before the light in your opponent's eyes extinguishes, but I *refuse* to stay in the car. This is my mess, so I'm going to help clean it up."

I won't make the same mistake I did two months ago. I tested the durability of the pocketknife I stuffed down my bra this time around. It shredded through a piece of uncooked steak like I stabbed it through a bowl of pudding. If one Petretti fails to come to the plate tonight for Maddox, a second one is at the ready.

"Demi—"

"No, Maddox. Our discussion is over. I am coming inside." He must hate the day he encouraged me to speak my mind because he's the only person I've used it on the past two months.

The scruffy beard he grew thanks to a lack of shaving equipment at the hospital does little to stop the moon's rays from bouncing off his teeth. He's smiling even while grumbling about me being a pain in his backside.

"For future reference, I much prefer when you bribe me with sex," he murmurs a couple of miles later.

Even though I squeeze his thigh, I keep my eyes on the road. "I'll be sure to remember that next time."

Our arrival at a warehouse on the outskirts of Erkinsvale doubles the frantic beat of my heart. Unlike my last arrival to a similar location, the parking lot isn't filled with foreign cars that fetch extremely high prices. Not even my uncle's Audi is here.

Maddox's eyes stray from the haunted-like warehouse to me when I rip open the glove compartment to pull out his wallet. It has details of tonight's fight stored inside of it, which is the very reason Maddox has kept it out of my sight all day.

I suck in a nerve-cleansing breath when the address on my uncle's business card matches the one Maddox input into the

GPS. I'm not relieved. I am hopeful tonight's event has been canceled.

Needing proof, I suggest for Maddox to go past the parking lot. "There's usually a back entrance to these types of places. My uncle likes showboating about his fighters while they make their way to the ring. He can't do that if they use the front entrance."

Wrongly believing I'm referencing him as one of my uncle's fighters, Maddox wrings the steering wheel.

That wasn't what I was doing. Not even close. I'd rather he not share the same air as my uncle, much less place Maddox in the same category as him.

"Dimitri will enter this way when he arrives." *If he arrives.* "There are no cameras."

I grow worried my uncle is up to something when we fail to stumble onto another vehicle near the back entrance of the warehouse. There are obvious tire tracks in the loose dirt, but not a single mode of transportation can be seen. It is as if everyone left in a hurry, and we're the only suckers left to face the fury alone.

"Where are all the cars?" Maddox asks, as suspicious as me.

"I don't know," I answer with a shrug. "Something feels wrong…" My words trail off when a familiar face pops out of the shadows under the awning of the warehouse. I frantically tap my hand on Maddox's forearm before adding a mangled roar to my unvoiced warning, "Go back!"

Before a single caution firing through Rocco's eyes can be decoded, the driver's side door of our car pops open, and Maddox's seat belt is removed with a knife.

He barely grunts, "What the fuck!" before he's dragged out

of his seat, thrown to the ground, then walloped with three brutal back-to-back hits to his face.

"Stop!"

After throwing off my seat belt, I toss open my door, then race around the hood of the car. I get within an inch of Maddox, who's being crushed by Dimitri's large frame when an arm bands around my waist, and I'm yanked back. "Let him blow off some steam."

Ignoring Rocco's recommendation, I fight him as Maddox is Dimitri. Maddox was caught by surprise, but once the shock wore off, he started giving as good as he is getting. He came prepared to fight tonight. He just had no clue his biggest battle would be in the parking lot.

When my fists don't talk on my behalf, I use words. "Let me go!" My command has scarcely left my mouth when Dimitri's fist causes blood to gush out of a wound above Maddox's left brow. "He's going to kill him."

Since Maddox was unprepared for Dimitri's onslaught, Dimitri has him at an advantage. He is straddling his lap, meaning every blow he inflicts is done to Maddox's head. Your brain can only rattle inside your skull so many times before it causes irreparable damage.

"He won't kill him. He's just gonna rough him up a bit. Let out some pent-up frustrations." Rocco's confirmation that my cousin only intends to beat my boyfriend won't stop me from punishing his ribs with my elbows. "He needs to learn his *place*." His last word comes out with a grunt when my kick to his shin loosens his grip on my waist enough I escape his clutch.

My hand stops creeping into my bra to remove the pocketknife when Dimitri screams into Maddox's face, "My daughter is *never* up for negotiation." *Daughter? I didn't know he had a daughter.* "If you *ever* try to use her again, not even she will be able to save you." He nudges his head to me during the 'she' part of his statement. "Do you understand me, Ox?"

My stomach launches into my throat when he finalizes his question with a faultlessly structured right swung hit to Maddox's temple. It should knock Maddox out. I've seen bigger men go down with a less potent punch, but all it does is encourage him to retaliate with just as much violence.

He slams his fist into Dimitri's ribs, grunts through a violent crack, then strays his eyes to mine. "Run!"

When I shake my head, shock rains down on Maddox before it's overcome by disappointment. He loathes that I'm ignoring the terms of our agreement, but they were negotiated for events *inside* the warehouse. There was no mention of what would occur outside of it.

While grunting through the pain of a possible cracked rib, Dimitri stands to his feet, dragging a stunned Maddox with him. After pinning him to the car like his body isn't aching from the beating Maddox subjected it to, he throws his fist into Maddox's unprotected face, leaving me no choice but to grab the gun stuffed down the back of his pants and aim it at the back of his head.

"Oh shit, Demi. What the fuck am I meant to do now?" Rocco chuckles out at the same time I tell Dimitri, "Let Maddox go, or I'll shoot you."

The gun rattles in my hand when Dimitri slowly slants his head my way. The exhaustion on his face reveals he's hurting as much as Maddox, but he doesn't understand the meaning of the word defeat. He'd fight to the death if he deemed it necessary.

After glaring at me long enough I'm certain he's scorched my skin, Dimitri shifts his narrowed, deadly eyes to Rocco. A word doesn't spill from his lips. However, it seems as if Rocco understands *exactly* which ones are screaming in his head.

"I can't, Dimi. I ain't got no beef with her." I can't see Rocco, but I picture him shuffling side to side like he's nervous when dust kicks up around my ankles. "Besides, it will teach you better gun management. I've told you that many times the past couple of ye—"

Quicker than I can blink, Dimitri snatches his gun out of my hand before stuffing the remainder of Rocco's comment into the back of his throat with a stern jab to the nose. It's clear Maddox watched me more than my cousin during high school when he seizes my wrist to tug me behind him in a protective stance. Dimitri is already pissed, so having a Petretti 'property' stolen out from beneath him directly in front of him will only make matters worse. A visiting professor at Seaforth Academy learned the hard way what happens when you try to claim ownership of something you don't own. Last I heard, he's teaching fish under gallons of salty water.

Ignoring both Rocco's chuckled assurance he'll get him back for his hit later, and Maddox's silent warning that he'd rather die than stand down as my protector, Dimitri locks his stern blue eyes with mine over Maddox's shoulder. His anger is at a pinnacle. The veins pulsating in his fisted hands are very telling, much less the tightness of his jaw, so you can imagine my shock when he says the last thing I anticipate for him to say. "You should have come to me sooner." His fists tighten even more when he drifts his eyes to the warehouse I'm certain his father was in at some stage today. My uncle's lingering aura can make my skin crawl even hours after he's left the room. "About *all* of it." He returns his eyes to me. "I could have helped you..." he pauses, swallows, then starts again, "I *can* help you."

He waits for me to nod in gratitude before he shifts on his feet to face Rocco. Once again, he doesn't speak, and once again, Rocco has no issue understanding him. "I'll update them as per your instructions... *all* parties included." Acting ignorant to the slightest bit of dribble of blood running out of his nose, he rubs his hands together like a kid eyeing a dozen presents under a Christmas tree. "Want me to pop a bullet in him while I'm at it?"

Dimitri's sigh is silent but very much noticeable. The rumble it causes his chest is compelling enough to shudder my toes. It's as powerful as the one I release when it dawns on me who they're talking about. I wish Rocco could take out my uncle as easily as he suggested it, but unfortunately, that would place his head on the chopping block in less than an hour.

"Don't mention her again." Dimitri's threatful words aren't for Rocco or me. They're for Maddox. "If you do..." He doesn't finalize his sentence. We all know what will happen if Maddox falls out of line. Tonight's punishment will seem like a walk in the park, and Dimitri will use more than fists during round two.

When Dimitri's eyes once again lock with mine, I dip my chin in farewell. It's cowardly for me to do, but no number of genie wishes could alter the facts. He showed restraint tonight. He is a killer in every meaning of the word. If he wanted Maddox dead, he would have shot him in the head within a nanosecond of pulling him out of the car.

Rocco was right. Dimitri's wrestle with Maddox tonight was merely about him blowing off some steam.

"What the fuck, Rocco?" Maddox breathes out heavily when Dimitri disappears into the shadows of a parking lot on the west side of the warehouse. "You were supposed to get him here on the pretense the people who have his daughter were in attendance, not fucking rat me out."

Woah. Hold on. What have I missed? Does someone have Dimitri's daughter?

Rocco smirks at my confused expression before stacking more turmoil onto my already overflowing plate. "If you think that's all he's keeping from you, keep asking questions, sister. That boy is a treasure trove of secrets."

His tongue peeks between his quirked lips when Maddox responds to his taunt with a tooth-bearing growl. "Start talking, Rocco, because I'm dying to hear your excuse." As Maddox steps up to him, he puffs his chest out. "That's how you operate, isn't it? Excuses by the bucketloads, and a fucked-up-enough childhood to get away with it."

The anger on Rocco's face reaches boiling point before he mutters, "You wanted a way out of tonight's fight."

"I wanted to get Demi and Sloane out of Col's grasp."

"And?" Rocco asks as if Maddox is slow. "That's what I've done, isn't it?" He barely nudges his head to the right an inch when the interior lights of a dark SUV illuminate, revealing a scared yet very much alive Sloane in the passenger seat.

Rocco stops my race for Sloane by seizing my wrist in a painless grasp, and just as quickly, Maddox shoves him back three places with a brutal shove, dislodging his hold. "I don't care who the fuck you are. Don't *ever* touch her without asking."

Violence isn't the solution for anything, but I'd be a liar if I said I didn't love Maddox's protectiveness. When I told him I hadn't been sexually assaulted by my uncle, he promised I would never be touched against my will. At the time, I thought he was issuing a promise he couldn't keep. Now I know better.

After adjusting his plain black shirt into place as if it is a tuxedo, Rocco responds to Maddox's shove with words instead of his fists. "Think wisely, my friend. You're burning bridges you can't rebuild."

Maddox acts as if his warning has no heat. "That bridge was burned a *long* time ago."

Certain they're moments from coming to blows, I step between them. Maddox isn't happy, but since it returns Rocco's focus to me, I'll handle his wrath at a more suitable time. "Why can't I see Sloane?"

While rubbing his hands together, Rocco's tongue delves out to replenish his lips. "She asked for a couple of minutes to get her head straight. Who am I to deny her request? When a girl has been through hell and back, you give them *everything* they ask for." He floats his eyes to Maddox, who's still glaring at him. "Am I right?" In Rocco's massively dilated eyes, I see Maddox lift his chin without pause for reflection. "And you'd take a beat down like a man to ensure her every want is answered, am I right?" When Maddox nods again, Rocco continues, "Then quit your fucking whining. Shit could have been way worse. Dimitri went lenient on you." He returns his eyes to me. "*Both* of you."

Although I am desperate to ask if Sloane specifically stated for me to be ousted from her self-reflection, I lose the chance when Rocco moves into the shadow of the awning he was camped under when we arrived to snatch up a gym bag—a gym bag that looks remarkedly similar to the one Maddox lost in the back of a cab.

Does that mean what I think it does? Was Agent Brahn working with Dimitri?

Surely not. He was too honest for that. Too straitlaced.

My deliberating is left for another day when Rocco tosses Maddox's gym bag onto the hood of the car Maddox borrowed from his fleet of many before he says, "Your first run is Monday. Dimitri trimmed them to three runs a week so you'll have plenty of time to prepare for fight night each week."

I'm curious to learn what Maddox is 'running' for Dimitri, but since I'm more concerned about what fight syndicate Dimitri has pre-scheduled for Maddox to participate in, I can't get my mouth to cooperate with the demands of my head.

After bouncing his eyes between two massively dilated pairs, Rocco adds, "Each *Friday* night fight." When Maddox and I exhale in sync, Rocco shifts on his feet to face me. "You need to be back on deck at Petrettis no later than next Friday. Dimi gave you some leeway due to your *situation*." The way he mutters 'situation' advises Dimitri is aware of my miscarriage. "This…" he strays his eyes over the derelict-looking warehouse that's eerily silent compared to how rowdy it usually is before adding, "… has cost Dimitri a pretty penny, so you need to pay him back."

In other words, he's saying I've been sold from my uncle to my cousin. Although I'd rather not be 'owned' by anyone, I much prefer being winged under my cousin's half of the Petretti entity than my uncle's. Dimitri is a mobster in every sense of the word, but I don't see incest ever being on his list of credentials.

"Col is aware of Dimitri's decision." My stomach gurgles so loud, I almost miss what Rocco says next. "He isn't happy, but he'll follow the rules. Maddox fought for Dimitri first. That put him on his payroll. You..." His facial expression looks torn between disgusted and angry. I realize it is both when he adds, "... should have *never* been up for negotiation, so with that in mind, Dimitri has agreed to pay you a salary for the hours you put in at Petretti's."

"I don't need his money..." My words trail off when Maddox squeezes my hand, wordlessly encouraging me to accept Rocco's offer. I'm lost as to why he wants me to take anything from my family, but I have to trust he wouldn't lead us down this path unless he deemed it necessary. "But it will be appreciated. Thank you."

Rocco smiles as if I offered him an invitation into my bed before he jerks his chin to the SUV I've barely taken my eyes off for the past two minutes. "Go say goodbye to your girl while we talk shop."

Although I hate being dismissed like I have no say about anything in my life, my wish to make sure Sloane is okay outranks anything else. Maddox is battered and bruised but still capable of taking down a tanker. Sloane looks seconds from collapse. I have to prioritize who needs me the most. Right now, that person is Sloane.

8

———

MADDOX

After waiting for Demi to be out of earshot, Rocco shoves a gym bag full of money into my chest. "I'm only going to tell you this once. If you run with this money, you're a dead man. Nothing I say or do will stop Dimi from hunting you down and gutting you like a fish."

"I won't steal from him. I'm not a complete fucking idiot." Since my reply is honest, it sounds that way.

"Nah, you just thought using his daughter as bait would fly." He calls me a fucking idiot under his breath before increasing the volume of his voice. "If you're not running, what's your plan?"

Don't be mistaken. He isn't asking a question, he's gauging a response. The angle of his head is a sure-fire sign of this, much less the way he stares at me like he has mindreading capabilities.

I stagger back in shock when he says a couple of seconds

later, "You're gonna stash away every bit of coin you can until you've got the funds to get her out of here." His chuckle vibrates both our chests when no number of unvoiced threats stop a shocked mask from slipping over my face. "You're not the first person to consider that, Ox. Won't be the last."

I'm still pissed about being ambushed without warning, but curiosity will always triumph a wish for revenge. "Have they ever gotten out?" I don't know why I'm seeking a score for my plan from a gangbanger. I could blame the rattle of my brain against my skull when Dimitri pummeled me with his fists, but I won't. I'm too cocky for that and way too fucking proud. Dimitri didn't walk away from our tussle uninjured. He was sporting as many bruises as me. It was just his body that got hammered instead of his head.

While kicking up rocks with his feet, Rocco shakes his head. I think all is lost until he breathes out slowly, "She did, though." He doesn't say a name, but I'm highly suspicious he's referencing Ophelia. His eyes have the same roguish glint they had when he showed me an up-to-date after-death photograph of her. "It was for the best. It's easier to hide one person than it is to hide two." I'm about to ask when he met Agent Brahn, but before I can, he continues talking, foiling my attempt. "Your plans will need to be placed on the backburner for a while. You can't leave until your debt is paid."

"Which will be only months away," I reply, equally pissed and confused.

Col shoved approximately twenty thousand into my chest after my first death-match. Even if that was only five percent of the pie, we're only in Dimitri's debt for four hundred thousand.

That seems like a lot, but at 10K a run, three runs a week, I'll have our debt paid off in a little over three months. Tack on another three months to put away some funds, we will be out of here long before Thanksgiving.

Rocco's chest-rattling laugh grates my last nerve. "You can't honestly believe you only need to pay Col out?" After spotting my answer in my eyes, he chuckles loud enough for Demi's focus to shift from Sloane to us. "That ain't close to the truth. Dimi is out of pocket over two million on ticket sales alone. Add another two million in lost bets, that brings you in a little over four million cool ones. Have you got that on you, Ox?" He digs his hand into my jacket before fanning it open. "I don't take checks without the Petretti name attached to them."

I slap his hands away from me before pushing him back with a shove. He finds it even more humorous than my scowl. He chuckles for several long seconds, his snickers only subsiding when a new way to piss me off enters his head.

"I know a way we could lessen your debt—"

"No." I shift on my feet to face Demi before signaling for her to come back. I hate ending her chat with Sloane before she's ready, but the longer we stay here, the more this grubby lifestyle will embed into my skin. Furthermore, Rocco's conversation with Dimitri hinted that Col is close by. That's an instant move-fucking-now command if I've ever heard one.

While shadowing my walk to the hanging open driver's side door Dimitri ripped me out of, Rocco says, "You didn't give me the chance to speak, so how could you possibly know what I was gonna say?"

I know *exactly* who he's referencing because his eyes got the same gleamy glint they get every time he rustles my feathers about Demi. A female member of my family is on his radar, but he isn't sniffing around for himself. He has Dimitri's six—*like he always does.*

I won't lie. My muscles scream like a bitch with every step I take, but since I'm confident Dimitri is feeling the same level of discomfort, I smirk instead of grimacing.

Mistaking my complacent face as one of consideration, Rocco tries to schmooze me. "It's the ideal solution, Ox. If you help Dimi get his girl back, he'll be in *your* favor. That's invaluable to any man."

"I said no, Rocco. Just like Fien isn't up for negotiation, neither is my sister." When shock flares through Rocco's eyes, stunned I knew his plan of attack, I mutter, "I'll find a way to pay Dimitri back. I just need—"

"Tweety birds to stop circling your head first?"

When I hit him with a stern sideways glare, his lips curl into a mammoth grin. He must have a death wish. Nothing rattles him, not even Dimitri's disappointment when he wouldn't pull his gun on Demi.

If it were anyone but Rocco denying Dimitri's every whim, I guarantee he'd be dead at my feet right now. Rocco has a way of getting through to Dimitri like no one else can. That's why I went to him with my plan instead of conjuring up my own way to get Dimitri onsite tonight. In a way, it worked. I was confident I'd have to fight tonight. I just never considered the possibility of Dimitri calling off the event before it happened.

After tossing the gym bag full of cash into the back seat, I lock my eyes with Rocco's. "Why did Dimitri cancel tonight's event?"

He rubs his hands together, a clear sign he's uncomfortable with the direction of our conversation. It won't stop him tattling, though. Rocco loves bragging. "It isn't just gangbangers who like seeing people get fucked up. *All* walks of life turn up to these events."

I nod, understanding what he's saying. Agent Moses didn't get footage of my first fight via magic. He was either ringside or was extremely chummy with someone who was. "Col is making mistakes—"

Before I can issue all of my warning, Rocco makes it clear he's aware of what it entails. "And Dimitri is tired of cleaning them up. It'll come to a head soon. Dimi just has more important things to focus on right now."

When I lift my chin in understanding for the second time, Demi slots into the passenger seat. She farewells Rocco with a dip of her chin because just like Dimitri, she's too pissed to give him a proper goodbye.

I'm halfway into the driver's seat, more than eager to get out of here before more controversy can be attached to my name when Rocco mutters, "If you change your mind about your sister, you know where to find me."

"I won't," I reply, my jaw tight.

I fire up the ignition, then rev the engine, drowning out Rocco's chuckles before I drift my eyes to Demi. I'm eager to leave but have no fucking clue where we're going. I thought we'd still be running. I didn't factor in the idea that Dimitri would ask for payment after shutting down his father's operation.

After watching Rocco climb into the driver's seat of the car Sloane is a passenger inside, Demi whispers five little words

I've been dying to hear her say for the past four days. "It's time to go home."

Halfway to Ravenshoe, I lean over the cab of the car to secure Demi's hand in mine. She's been noticeably quiet since we left the warehouse. I haven't minded. It gave me plenty of time to un-muddle my confusion, then a couple of minutes to plan our next move. It still involves getting Demi as far away from her uncle as possible. It's just going to take a little longer than I'd hoped.

"How was Sloane?" I ask, desperate to strike up a conversation. Demi hasn't been this quiet since Landon said her entire family should be sterilized so their bloodline would become extinct.

Demi strays her eyes from the scenery whizzing by her window to me. "She's okay. A little shaken but mostly unharmed. She asked me to give this to Saint." She shows me a handwritten note on the back of a boutique-shop receipt.

"Is she going somewhere?" I question, surprised Sloane wouldn't give her note to Saint herself. She's pretty ballsy. I didn't think anything would faze her.

The reason for Demi's quiet smacks into me when she briefly bobs her head. "She got an offer a couple of months back to study abroad. She initially turned it down..."

"*This* changed her mind?" I fill in when her voice cracks too much for her words to be legible.

Demi nods again. "It will be good for her. I'm happy for her and all that. I'm just going to miss her."

I raise her hand to my mouth, kiss it, then nibble on the edge of it. I'm not making light of the situation. I am simply doing everything in my power to stop Demi's tears from falling. She hates when she cries. Her dislike has nothing on the aversion I feel, though.

When my touch doesn't fully eradicate the groove between her brows, I throw words into the mix. "Maybe we can visit her one day?"

Demi's eyes drop to her hands in her lap before she mumbles something about how she'd need a passport first.

"Then we'll get you one." I wait for her eyes to lock with mine before adding, "There's an entire world out there waiting to be explored. Why can't it be explored by us?"

I eye her curiously when she unexpectedly smiles. I was endeavoring to weaken the tension between us, but I would have never predicted a grin. Don't get me wrong. I'm glad crying is now the last thing on her mind. I'm just super curious to learn what changed between now and five minutes ago.

"What's got you smiling?" I ask, too curious for my own good.

"Nothing important."

Her smile doubles when I gawk at her, loathing that she's leaving me hanging. I often blurt out the wrong thing at the most inappropriate time because I'm so damn impatient. I'd rather stick my foot in my mouth than wait for a better reply.

Only once I'm on the verge of begging does Demi finally surrender up the goods. "I was just wondering if that's the excuse my uncle will run with when he spends the next six months in Italy."

"He's going abroad?" I ask my question so loud, I'm certain three blocks over hear it.

Demi's grin turns blinding. "Around twenty minutes after Dimitri arrived, Sloane overheard Col telling his associates that he was needed on urgent business matters." She air quotes her last two words. "He will be gone until at least Labor Day."

Although her happiness makes me happy, we need to remain cautious. We did have a win tonight. It may not seem like it when I'm running coke from town to town, but compared to what I was prepared to face, you could class it as a victory. I just need the knot in my stomach to get the message. It's holding on firm like the worst is still to come.

When I say that to Demi, she squeezes my thigh. "I know. I feel sick to my stomach as well, but it will be nice not needing to look over our shoulders all the time. The apple doesn't fall far from the tree, but with Dimitri's focus devoted to finding his daughter, I don't see him having the time to meddle in our affairs."

Loathing that my inability to look a gift horse in the mouth is stealing the joy from Demi's face, I bring out the coping mechanism I always use when feeling snowed under. "You only spoke with Sloane for ten minutes, so how the fuck did you cover so much ground?"

Demi smiles in a way I was certain I'd never witness again before she mutters, "You have no idea." As quickly as her smile arrived, it fades away. She doesn't appear upset. Maiming seems more on the agenda when she asks, "How come you didn't tell me Dimitri has a daughter… a *missing* daughter?"

"In all honesty, I forgot about her until we bumped into Col this morning." I pause, aware my next set of words will most likely hurt Demi, but since I need them to explain myself, I have no choice but to express them. "The innocence in Sloane's eyes when she was pushed out of Col's car hit me with a truckload of things at once... both past and present."

Demi slowly nods like she too was bombarded. "It made me think about Kaylee, and if my uncle's claim about killing her was true. It was obvious he hated my father, but he seemed to have a weird fondness for my mother, so why would he hurt her like that?"

I wish I had an answer for her. I simply don't.

"Some people's logic can't be explained," I say a short time later. "You'll become as unhinged as them just striving to work them out." That's my nice way of saying she shouldn't waste her breath on her uncle. Nothing she can do or say will bring Kaylee back, so she needs to concentrate on what she can change, starting with her own safety. "Things will probably be a little crazy when we rock up. I've never vanished without a trace before, not to mention returning with a ghost." I moisten my lips before asking, "Are you sure this is what you want? I'm happy to continue hiding if you think it is for the best."

"I'm sure," Demi replies without hesitation. "The only person I needed to hide from was my uncle." Her expression is a cross between disappointed and angry when she continues, "He already knows I'm alive, so..." She finalizes her reply with a shrug.

That's true. I don't like it, but I can't change it.

"I just hope your family will be okay with me showing up unannounced." She fixes the hem on her dress like it wasn't already perfect. "I don't want to give them an excuse to dislike me more than they already do."

"They don't dislike you." When she rolls her eyes, I talk faster. "They don't, Demi. You didn't see their faces when Dr. Falgar said you were…" I stop with barely a second to spare. My voice almost cracked. "They were devastated. Caidyn punched a tree. He never does that. He fuckin' loves trees."

Her giggle is a nice thing to hear during an oxygen-depriving conversation. "I thought he was mad at me. Our chats became less frequent the more times he babysat me."

I shake my head to hide my breathy sigh. "Did he happen to spend a lot of time on his phone?" Demi appears lost to where I'm going with this, but she nods her head, nonetheless. "Did you happen to snoop over his shoulder at *any* stage during his 'babysitting' slots?"

She whacks me in the arm for overemphasizing my babysitting comment before she once again shakes her head. "I'm not a stalker, Maddox… *unlike you.*"

I chuckle, happy to wear the title with pride, especially when it comes to her. "Since this is Caidyn we're talking about, the next time you see him tapping wildly on the screen of his phone, take a peek at who he's talking to. Saint and Landon are fans of dick pics. Caidyn prefers perfectly staged selfies."

Even though Demi giggles again, she doesn't deny my claims. Anyone who has met Caidyn knows two of his best assets are his jawline and unique colored eyes. He woos them with his dick *after* the obligatory third date.

"Caidyn would never hate you, Demi. He doesn't understand the meaning of the word. Saint will kiss your ass for the next ten weeks as he strives to work out a way to fix that…" I nudge my head to the receipt she's clutching. "And Justine…" I smile while recalling the texts we shared when she found out I was shacked up at our family cabin with Demi. "She thinks the world of you because she knows you make me happy."

Demi's eyes glisten with happiness, but something is dulling them. Or should I say, 'someone?'

"And Landon?" Demi asks, her tone reserved. "What's your take on him?"

I wring the steering wheel for a couple of seconds while endeavoring to work out a reason for Landon's analness. He's the more conservative one of the Walsh siblings, and he's quick to jump to conclusions, but he's only been that way the past three years.

"Landon fell in love with the wrong woman." Curiosity crosses Demi's features, but her lips don't utter a syllable. "She was thirteen years his senior, married, and his college professor."

"Oh…" Demi breathes out slowly after stacking the chips into a messy pile.

"Yeah, *oh.* Shit hit the fan when I wasn't the only one who walked in on them doing extracurricular *activities* after class."

Like all women who love gossip, Demi's eyes light up like a Christmas tree. "You knew about their affair?"

I jerk up my chin. "I warned Landon that it would end badly." Oddly, I used the same words Landon used on me when he tried to caution me about staying away from Demi. I just didn't use ditch or jail metaphors in my reply. Well, I did use jail, but that was more in reference to his professor than him. "He ignored my warning. Turned out I wasn't far off the mark."

"What happened to her?"

I stray my eyes from the road to Demi. "The professor?"

When she nods, I shrug. "I don't know. Although universities encourage faculty to see students as scholars instead of sexual partners, no laws were broken." My brows pull together as guilt makes itself known with my stomach. "I assumed she moved to another university, but I don't have solid proof."

My comment makes me realize I let Landon down. The bro-code states we're supposed to have each other's back no matter what, so how is it he had his heart broken without any of his brothers' support?

"Maybe you should ask Landon what happened to her?" Demi recommends like she's not suggesting for me to open a big ass can of worms.

"Even after this long?"

She nods. "If I were you, I'd be asking. The length of their relationship doesn't matter. It's the quality of the time that went into it that counts. You said Landon loved her. To him, that makes her unforgettable."

Fuck, my girl is smart. She's considerate too. Even when her focus should be on herself, she forever places the needs of others above her own. It's a quality I love about her as much as I hate it. If she weren't this way, my family would have been on her uncle's radar years sooner than we were, back when we weren't as equipped to protect ourselves. If she had occasionally placed herself first, perhaps things wouldn't have gotten as bad as they did.

It's hard to truly know. Col's arrogance seems to feed on Demi's fight, so I could be wrong. If she had fought, Col might have pushed back just as firmly. I refuse to consider what the outcome of that tussle could have been. It guts me hearing stories of Demi's teenage years. I don't want to throw a heap of 'what ifs' into the mix.

After pulling down a very familiar street, I stray my eyes to Demi. "If Landon becomes too much, let me know. I'll pull him into line." Even in the dark, I notice how dilated her eyes become when I add, "Or perhaps you can with the pocketknife you snuck into your bra during supper."

9

DEMI

I drift my eyes to Maddox when he says, "Don't be nervous."

He can say that because he's returning to the land of the living after taking a 'breather' for four days.

I'm resurrecting from the dead.

That isn't the cause of my panic, though. It's striving to work out how the Walshs will react when they discover Maddox's disappearance is my fault.

I love the Walshs. I've strived to emulate their family dynamic for years in everything I do, but I don't see them being overly obliging about me intruding on their reunion.

I'm an outsider.

An outcast.

Even more so now since Sloane has decided to study abroad for the last two years of her studies. I understand where her decision stems from, I just wish it could have been *wholly* her choice. No one should be scared out of their home. My family home was bland and uninviting, but if I had the choice, I would have stayed there for a lifetime.

Forever on alert when it comes to my teetering emotions, Maddox curls his hand around mine before giving it a gentle squeeze. "You ready?"

I peer at him, smiling when I notice his eyes. Although swollen and bruised from Dimitri's beat down, they don't have the slightest bit of green to them. This is his home, and he's ecstatic I am here with him. The knowledge settles my nerves in an instant.

"I'm ready," I reply with a brisk nod.

With his spare hand, he drags his index finger down my nose before he lowers the handle on the front door of his childhood home. It's almost midnight, however, the late hour doesn't detract from the familiar sound of a police radio booming into my ears when we enter the elaborate foyer. Just the entrance of the Walsh family residence is bigger than the living room of my childhood home. It's decorated as if Mrs. Walsh is an interior designer, not an architect for a massive firm that does everything from skyscrapers in New York to environmental landscapes in the Bahamas.

"We're doing everything we can, Mrs. Walsh, but you must understand, Maddox's text has officers apprehensive that this is a missing person case," cautions a female voice that's laced with apprehension. Her tone alone advises she doesn't believe Maddox will return anytime soon, and I'm not the only one who notices.

"His bank accounts haven't been touched in days. His motorbike was last seen in a region of the state no one in our family has heard about. My boy wouldn't just up and vanish like this."

Mr. Walsh's crackling voice breaks my heart. He is the reason the Walsh brethren is so protective of those they love. He is the commander of their realm. He doesn't rule with cruel, undermining tactics like my tyrant of an uncle does, though. He nurtures his children when needed and wallops them up the back of the head when they step out of line.

"He's hurting, which means he needs his family more than anything."

Hearing the fret in his father's voice as readily as me, Maddox coughs, wordlessly announcing our arrival. His father spins around so quickly, I grow worried he'll think I'm an illusion. There's no way he isn't dizzy.

"Maddox," his mother mutters on a sob before she leaps up from her chair and races across the room.

Even with it being the weekend, every member of Maddox's immediate family is in the living room—his parents, brothers, and sister. Even a handful of his aunts I haven't seen in over a decade have their backsides planted in a chair.

They spill to our side of the room one by one, their joy about Maddox's return too strong to be dampened by a heap of questions neither Maddox nor I are willing to answer just yet.

They cuddle Maddox, noogie his head, cry into his neck, then move onto me to do the same. My hair doesn't get messed by their hands, though. They cradle my jaw while endeavoring to wipe away tears that shouldn't be falling. There are no bullies in this room. I just struggle to understand that sometimes it's okay to cry. Not all tears are sad ones. Tonight's are most certainly not.

The room falls into silence when the two people left in the living room remain on their side, guarded by silence. The African American police officer's apprehension is understandable. To her, Maddox's 'disappearance' was a waste of police resources. He's a hothead who exploited her time because he wasn't 'feeling it,' but Landon's withdrawn composure is unexpected. Not for me—it's clear I'll never be in his good books—but for Maddox. They left things on bad terms the last time they spoke, but he wouldn't be here if he weren't worried about Maddox. Shouldn't that speak for something?

I smile in gratitude when the officer breaks the intense standoff first. She doesn't race for Maddox like the rest of the Walsh clan did. She apprehensively makes her way to me, her eyes puzzled and brimming with panic. "You're... *ah*. You are—"

"Demi Petretti," I introduce when she struggles to speak through the fear clutching her throat. "It's a pleasure to meet you." I thrust out my hand, aware I tarnished our greeting by using my full name, but I'm at a point in my life where I need to stop being ashamed of who I am.

My family name is dirty.

I am not.

And although I pray like hell my children will never know the burden of carrying my last name, nothing I can do will change the fact they will have the Petretti genes and DNA.

"Demi..." The officer smiles in a way that would have you convinced her heart isn't breaking before she dips her chin in farewell. "I must go."

Several pairs of eyes snap to mine when she makes a beeline for the door like I threatened her very existence with a tiny introduction. When I shrug, truly unsure what made her upset, Mrs. Walsh chases her down. "Regina, wait!"

With the tension in the room at boiling point, Landon crosses it without so much of an eye on him. He stands across from his baby brother with his hands balled at his sides and his eyes bouncing between the older members of his family.

Just when his anger appears to be cooling, he raises one of his fists and socks Maddox in the eye like it isn't already swollen.

"Landon!" Justine shouts when Maddox sails into the entryway table with a thud.

I don't know if it's my inability not to flinch when confronted with violence or Mr. Walsh's stern warning that Landon better get himself in check, but whatever it is, I am as shocked as hell when Landon's response to my resurrection doesn't arrive with the same level of violence he hit Maddox with. He pulls me into his chest before pressing his lips to the top of my head. He doesn't say anything. He doesn't need to. His raging heart tells me everything I need to know. He's happy I'm here, he just couldn't let his baby brother get away with hurting his parents so viciously. He had to respond. It's in the Walsh DNA.

"Ice his eye, calm him down as only you can, then have him call me," Landon requests after drawing me back to an arm's length. He waits for me to nod before he nudges his head to the stairwell behind us. "Some of his belongings are still in his room. I put a bag of clothes in there for you as well. If you need anything else, reach out."

I nod again, too choked up by his words to formulate a response. As far as he was aware, I was dead. So why did he bring some of my things here for me? Did he know I was alive? Or did he realize I'm the only person capable of stealing Maddox away from his family?

After a final gaze at his family, Landon drops his hands from my shoulders, then exits via the same door Officer Regina and Mrs. Walsh bolted through. It takes me hearing Maddox telling Justine he's fine before I click that he was assaulted for the second time tonight. I have no doubt he could have responded to Landon's anger with just as much aggression. He chose not to because despite what he will tell you, our conversation during our drive to Ravenshoe now has him more empathetic on who Landon is and why he is the way he is.

"What did he say?" Maddox asks me from his station on the floor, his words muffled by the tea towel Justine is holding under his nose.

Memories of the time he defended me against my first bully not related to me filter through my head when I kneel in front of him to check if his nose is still bleeding. "He said to ice your eye before taking you upstairs to have my wicked way with you."

Maddox freezes for all of two seconds before the truth falls around him. "He brought our things here?" We've been together twenty-four seven for a majority of the past two months, but I still get giddy when he says 'our.'

When I nod, Maddox leaps to his feet like his head isn't the slightest bit woozy. "What did I tell you, Demi? My family loves you."

Embarrassed he spilled one of my most guarded secrets to the very people I wanted to keep it hidden from, I stray my eyes among the members of his family gawking at me. I'm not exactly sure how to explain the look they're giving me. It's a cross between disappointed and remorseful but with a hint of admiration attached to it like they're pleased I care about their opinion enough to express it out loud.

"It isn't that I thought you hated me. I just thought perhaps maybe you'd..."

"Discriminate you because of your family name?" Justine fills in when my words fade to silence. "If you believe that, Maddox has done a poor job advocating the Walsh traits." She narrows her eyes into thin slits before drifting them to Maddox. "But I guess it wouldn't be the first time someone in this family has jumped to conclusions." She doesn't mention Dimitri's name, but the scorn on her brothers' faces fills in the gap.

"They have good reasons for their worry."

Justine doesn't hear my reply. I'll be surprised if she hears anything after the ear-bashing Saint and Caidyn hit her with. They take one ear each, harping on about how their mom is going to design the ivory tower Saint, Caidyn, and Maddox plan to build and how Landon will have the only key.

I divert my eyes from a red-faced Justine when Maddox's tattooed arm brushes against my shoulder. "That went better than expected." When I slowly crank my neck back to Justine, who looks on the verge of screaming, he pushes out with a laugh, "We could save her, but then the focus would be back on us." Our topsy-turvy day should stop the curving of my knees when he adds, "Which means we couldn't head upstairs to wash off the funk of our day. You still smell as scrumptious as fuck, but I'm feeling a little grubby." He licks his lips before breaking them into an insanely sexy grin. "So, what do you say, Demi?

Should we save Justine, or would you rather wash my back after I wash yours?"

I'm a terrible person when I slip my hand into his before tiptoeing us toward the stairwell like Mr. Walsh isn't mere feet from the landing, watching Mrs. Walsh's exchange with the ashen-faced police officer, but not even a massacre could stop my body from responding to the need in Maddox's voice.

He changed who he was for me, so the least I can do is ensure he always comes first.

MADDOX

"Hold your gun properly. Your arm is wobbling." Acting ignorant to the lowering of Demi's brows as she scolds me through her protective equipment, I raise her arm back to its original position before taking a quick glance down the barrel of her gun.

Only four short weeks ago, we gave the experts something to laugh at during their time at the range. Now, Demi has so much accuracy lining up her targets, I remind her for the fourth time today *never* to point her gun at anything she doesn't want dead.

"I'll never shoot you, Maddox..." I wait, knowing there's more, "... unless you start taking dating advice from Saint. That warrants at least a bullet graze."

Although I agree with her, I pretend as if I don't know what she's talking about. "Ouch... what did Saint ever do to you?"

When she spins to face me, the fake concern on my face

shifts to pride. She immediately angled her gun away from me, and her finger moved off the trigger even quicker than that.

Safe gun practices are a good skill to learn, not only for confidence but for personal protection as well. What Sloane overheard weeks ago was true. Demi's uncle commenced a six-month paid 'vacation' to Sicily the day after Dimitri ambushed me at the warehouse. He is thousands of miles away, which should make his ability to hurt Demi almost impossible, but he isn't the only monster in our closet. Rogue agents like Arrow Moses are still hiding in the dark, waiting for the perfect opportunity to jump out and startle us. He's subdued now since I increased my runs with Dimitri from three a week to six, but I doubt that will be the case once my debt has been repaid and truths are shared in a career-ending tell-all.

Tattlers always end up dead, but since that's precisely the story I'm planning to run with when Demi and I leave the country, I have every intention of taking Agent Moses down with me.

Until then, nothing but ensuring Demi's mental health and well-being is maintained is on my mind. I'll even let her throw daggers at my brothers if it keeps her spirits up.

"He let her go, Maddox."

"Saint didn't let Sloane go." I watch her trigger finger to ensure there's no twitch before finalizing, "He *accepted* her decision as our father taught us." I'm a prick for adding my father's teachings into our conversation but tell me you wouldn't do the same if it ends an argument even faster than it began. "If you don't have to walk in the shoes of the person making the decision *after* they've made it, the decision is not yours to make. Sloane wanted to go abroad—"

"Because she was scared."

Although I'd rather not bicker about a relationship I'm not involved in, I'll take one for team Walsh today. "Scared of who, *exactly*?"

As her brows pull together, Demi freezes. "My uncle. Who else would she be scared of?"

I twist my lips. "I can think of at least one more person."

She exhales a sharp, warning breath. "I have no clue who you're talking about." Her diva-like attitude gains her the attention of numerous sets of eyes. "Dimitri and Rocco helped her, so she'll forever see them as her saviors, and you, I'm not exactly sure what she thinks of you, but I'm reasonably sure she isn't scared of you."

The jealousy blazing through her eyes won't stop me from nibbling at the bait she threw out. "Dem—" Her twitching trigger finger cuts me off. Not enough to keep me down for the count, but enough I hold my hands out in front of me in a non-threatening manner before taking a step closer to her. "She heard Col was going abroad. She knew he couldn't hurt her, not just because you would have never let her out of your sight, but neither would have Saint. She left because—"

"She fell in love with a man who swore never to fall in love." As she sucks in an angry breath, her finger taps the barrel on her gun. "Who makes a pledge like that? Even my uncle, a heartless tyrant of a man, has been in love. If he can do it, why can't Saint?"

"I don't know." I lower my hand to her gun, sighing softly when she gives up her deadly weapon without too much protest. "But Saint's inner-workings don't interest me." After placing her gun next to mine, I tug off her earmuffs and protective glasses before dragging my index finger down her nose. It instantly subdues her. "Yours, however, very much do."

With the sexual chemistry between us at a pinnacle, Demi crowds in close to ensure her next set of words are only for my ears. "Stay with me tonight. Skip this shipment." We haven't directly spoken about what I 'run' for Dimitri, but her father didn't keep her out of the family 'business' enough for her not to put two and two together. "We could go to the Walsh family cabin. I'll cook for you, then we could play a board game."

My cock immediately stiffens from the husky deliverance of her last sentence. I, however, act ignorant. "I can't skip tonight's run." I don't give a fuck that Rocco would ride my ass for weeks on end for pulling out of a shipment at the last minute. Denying Demi's offer has nothing to do with drugs and everything to do with a surprise I've kept secret the past three weeks. "But I did switch up next week's roster so I can watch you cook at Petretti's Saturday night. Perhaps once you've finished there, we could go to the cabin?"

She groans instead of moaning as I was hoping. "You don't come to Petretti's to marvel at my culinary skills, Maddox. Admiration and stalking are two very different things."

"I don't stalk you." *I fucking do, at all times of the day and night.* "I'm keeping an eye on you. Just because your uncle is out of town doesn't mean it isn't business as usual at Hopeton."

Having no plausible defense to my accurate statement, Demi returns her earmuffs to their original position, pops back on her protective glasses, then grabs her gun off the bench at our side. The hardness I experienced earlier returns full force when she plants her feet at the width of her shoulders, holds her arms high and firm, then fires three times at the paper silhouette.

My cock should shrivel like my grandma walked in on me stroking my schlong when her third shot blows out the paper guy's crotch. It doesn't, though. There's nothing sexier than a girl who can protect herself, so I won't mention the tiny shorts she's wearing or how she pulled her hair back in a sexy pair of pigtails, knowing it does crazy things to me. If I mention those things, I'll walk funny for a week.

Even with us staying at my parents' place—they've developed displacement issues since I went missing, so moments like today are a rarity—Demi's sexual appetite returned to what it was before Landon flung a heap of steaming shit onto her family name. She isn't as vocal as I'd like when she rides my face like a carousel at a fair, but with my family home having bathrooms for each bedroom and them being in opposing corners of the somewhat mansion-size house, the restraints are becoming less restrictive with each day that passes. We will go back to the cabin one day, just not until I'm as convinced as Demi that the worst is behind us.

My tongue peeks between my teeth when Demi finalizes her round by blowing on the end of her gun like smoke is pluming from the barrel. She has missed Sloane like crazy the past four weeks, but sparks of the Demi I knew before she was shipped from foster home to foster home is shining brightly. She'll never be at full contentment—I don't know one orphan who would—but I'm working like crazy to ensure she gets damn close to the happiness she felt when her father was still around.

"You fuckin' love that you've got all the men around us mentally checking that they still have their packages, don't you?" I stray my eyes across the men happy to gawk from a distance but way too scared to consider approaching Demi like they did her first couple of sessions here.

They said to my face that they thought it was 'cute' I wanted her to know how to protect herself, then straight up told Demi she wouldn't need to know how to fire a gun if she was with them.

It's safe to say that was when Demi's love of making men squirm was founded. She's taken out the nuts of every paper silhouette ever since.

While dragging her teeth over her bottom lip, Demi locks her roguish eyes with mine. "It's more fun than making them come in their pants."

I angle my head and arch a brow, portraying that I'm annoyed at her inability to make men come simply by looking at them. It's all an act. Everyone can be a superhero. Some fight baddies for a living, others make people orgasm with a smile, and mine is realizing my kryptonite is also my biggest weapon. She has the ability to kill me, but instead of using her powers against me, she gives me the strength to fight with her.

I went through with Agent Moses's suggestion because I wanted to do some good for my community. Some may believe my plans fell off the wagon when I killed a man. I don't see it that way. My objectives haven't changed. I am doing good for my community because if Demi can escape the carnage she was born into, perhaps her fight will encourage others to do the same.

Hopeton's downfall isn't because of the bad things Demi's uncle has done to its residents. It is because of the silence of the good ones. If more people spoke out against violence and discrimination, Col wouldn't have gotten away with as much as he has.

"Huh?" I mutter when Demi waves her hand in front of my face.

She smiles in a way that forever reminds me her smiles are by far my most favorite. "Were you daydreaming about me naked again?"

This time around, I *doink* her nose instead of running my finger down it. "Not this time around, but thanks for the reminder that I'm due for a refresher." I nudge my head to the locker rooms not even I would shower in without shoes. "Do you want to head out back for a private lesson?"

Demi's smile switches to a giggle when I make *pew-pew* noises with my mouth while gesturing my head to the crotch of my pants—the *extended* crotch since I'm imagining firing blanks down Demi's throat.

"A double business major and you still think of your cock as a pistol." She rolls her eyes hoping it will stop her smile from ruining her ruse that she's annoyed. "Forewarning, if you call your cock a doodle at any stage, I'm out."

I chuckle until the entirety of her reply smacks into me. "Does that mean you're in?"

Good gun safety is the last thing on my mind when the replenishing of Demi's suddenly dry lips answers my question on her behalf. It's not close to Christmas, but I'm reasonably sure all my Christmases are about to come at once.

MADDOX

The clamminess of nightmare-coated skin makes my fingertip jut across Demi's temple instead of smoothly sliding across it when I pull her hair back from her face. I'm still suffering nightmares like a soft cock who's never had his dick sucked, but since they have nothing to do with Igor, and everything to do with the girl of my dreams dying before me, they don't annoy me like they did after Igor's death.

I hate waking up drenched in sweat and unable to breathe, but it only takes the quickest trace of Demi's fingertips over the bumps in my midsection to remind me Dr. Falgar's words were a ruse, a ploy to take Demi away from me. She's here, in my family's home, seemingly safe, but I'll never truly believe she's fully out of harm's way until there are more than twenty miles between Hopeton and her.

"Stay asleep," I whisper when Demi stirs. "I didn't want to head out without saying goodbye." I'll never forgive myself for how I ran out on her that morning at the cabin. What if that had been the last time I saw her? I didn't even say goodbye.

I smile against Demi's lips when they find mine in the darkness of the night. She's groggy from the late hour we crashed last night, and the sweaty mess I woke in altered my smell from the familiar shower gel slash Demi combination she's used to, but she still finds my mouth no matter how poor the conditions.

"Please be careful," she whispers over my lips, conscious it's never too early for criminal activities.

"I will. I love you."

"I love you back," she murmurs through a yawn, stealing my line.

I weave my fingers through her dark hair for another two minutes before slipping into the hallway. I make it to the landing of the stairwell when a faint giggle stops me in my tracks. It's five in the morning. It isn't a giggle-appropriate hour.

With our house specifically designed for privacy, it doesn't take me long to realize which room the giggle came from. The entire family is home for our parents' wedding anniversary dinner, including Justine. Although she could be talking to one of the many suitors Landon, Caidyn, and Saint have yet to scare off, my gut is cautioning me not to be so stupid.

After praying like fuck Rocco is a patient man, I walk away from the staircase instead of galloping down it. Justine barely mumbles a syllable when I squash my ear up against her door. I assume that's because the person she's speaking with doesn't let her get in a word—even more incriminating evidence that she's talking to someone she shouldn't be—but am proven wrong when her bedroom door flies open a couple of seconds later. Her bedroom light is off, and the chandelier above the stairwell is never turned off. She would have seen my shadow under the door.

"It's impolite to eavesdrop on private conversations." She strays her eyes to a door that's rarely open—the door to my childhood bedroom. "I thought you'd know that better than anyone."

Since her voice is more pitched with amusement than anger, I get cheeky. "I do. Why do you think I bought everyone noise-canceling headphones for Christmas?"

When she misses the punch line, Justine rolls her eyes. "You lived at the cabin when you bought those. That's miles from here."

She looks torn between gagging and high-fiving me when I say, "Trust me, a stallion's neighs can be heard for miles. Even Caidyn won't deny that."

When I gallop like a horse, she socks me in the stomach. Her movements cause the screen of her cell phone to illuminate, exposing she didn't end her call, she merely took an intermission. "You're disturbing."

"Says the person who's up before the sparrows being sweet-talked into a booty call. Is that Brax?"

Justine puts more *oomph* into her hit this time around. "No, it isn't Brax, and it also isn't a booty call." She whispers her words, not only to ensure the rest of her overbearing brothers don't hear her but her caller as well. The way she covered the speaker with her hand is a sure-fire sign of this, much less her white-knuckle grip. "It's a friend."

"A friend? *Right.*" I'm about to demand she hand over her

phone, but a brilliant idea pops into my head long before Justine's frustrated screams can come close to waking the dead. "If it's *just a friend*, then they won't mind you calling them back in a couple of hours. I need a favor."

"*You* need *my* help?"

I take a moment to relish the shock in her voice before jerking up my chin. I had planned to do a run for Dimitri before spending the remainder of my morning working on the surprise I'm planning for Demi, but I'm willing to switch things up if it has Justine dissing her caller.

After holding her finger in the air, requesting a minute, Justine squashes her cell phone against her ear. "Can I call you back?" She sheepishly peers at me through thick lashes before saying, "Everything's fine. He just needs my help with something." I can't hear the person she's talking to, but I know it's a man. Justine doesn't do gaga eyes at anyone but our father, but whatever her caller replies with has her eyes gleaming with more than happiness. "I will. Bye."

I begin to doubt my theory when the lowering of her phone from her ear has me spotting the length of her call. She's been talking for over four hours. I don't care how in touch with your feminine side you are, no guy talks for four hours straight *unless* they're desperate for a piece of the pie.

I swallow down the vomit scorching my throat when Justine asks if she has time to change. "I'll wait for you out front."

Confident I have an easy ten minutes to waste, I take the stairs one at a time instead of galloping down them like I usually do. As prearranged, Rocco meets me by the side gate. He's dressed like his day is only starting, even with the rings under his eyes saying otherwise. After tossing my gym bag into my chest, he says, "Same deal as yesterday, except I need you to weigh the bricks today. Quantities are right, but the bricks seem a little light."

"I'm not weighing coke for you," I fire back, mortified he'd even suggest it. "As far as anyone is aware, I'm moving bags of flour between bakeries."

Rocco grins at the disgust in my tone. I still hate what I do, but he knows I'd rather run drugs for him than be Col or Agent Moses's lacky. "I'm not asking you to test the merchandise, fuckface. I just need you to check the digits on a set of scales before they load the bricks into the trunk." Unwilling to take no for an answer, he shoves a prototype tablet into my chest. "Weight specifications are on here. If you have any issues…" He taps his index finger on a business card stuffed under the protective casing of the tablet. The lack of information on the card tugs my lips into a smirk. It has nothing but a cell phone number smack bang in the middle of a piece of black-gilded cardboard.

"What if the scales are off?"

Rocco rubs his hands together before he breaks out his biggest grin to date. "Leave with the goodies, then ring me. I'll send some men over for a tea party." His smile sags when the creak of a front door opening buzzes louder than the mosquitoes circling our heads. "Expecting company?"

I cut off his reach for his gun with a warning sideways glance. "It's my sister."

I have more understanding of the benefits of carrying a weapon when Rocco's smile returns like it never left. Except this time, it isn't laced with stirring. It's poisoned with envy. "Perhaps I should chaperone this run. I wouldn't want anything to happen to the supposedly untouchable Justine Walsh."

"I've got a handle on things," I assure him for the umpteenth time the past five weeks. Although this is the first time he has used Justine to rile me instead of Demi, it doesn't see me offering him any leeway. "I'm also not taking my baby sister on a drug run. That may be how things work with your family, but the Walshs don't operate that way."

"Says you."

With Justine galloping down the palatial front stairs of our family home, I don't have the time nor the care to reply to his mumbling comment. Instead, I give him a look, one that announces it's time for him to fuck off.

"The merchandise will be on deck long before fight night commences," I guarantee when the business side of Rocco's head switches on. He's all fun and games until it comes with a risk of lost revenue.

"No later than five, Ox. Don't make me come searching for you." He tosses me the keys for his Buick a mere second before he disappears into the darkness of a shadow.

Justine is at my side a nanosecond after the revs of his Mercedes G Class fade to a buzz. "I should have brought my coat. The winds whipping off the ocean are a little chilly." That's her way of saying she's suspicious about why we're creeping out of the house at five in the morning.

As far as she is aware, Demi and I disappeared because we got into a fight. I took off for a few days to 'get over her' and only returned once I realized that would never happen.

I was pissed when I found out the stories our brothers told her while I was away. I get they wanted to save her the heartache of knowing the truth, but surely, walking around with a blindfold on is worse than a tiny nick to an unvital artery.

The wary gleam hueing Justine's cheeks double when I gesture for her to climb into the passenger seat of the Buick. My family has seen me getting around in Rocco's ride a couple of times the past five weeks, but they have no clue where it came from or why it shows up unannounced.

I switch on the radio before slinging my eyes to my baby sister. "Your playlist or mine?"

Justine's innocence is showcased without fault when she screws up her nose at my suggestion. "Duh. Mine, of course. I can't understand any of the words in the songs you play. All they do is scream. That is *not* singing."

Even with her having a point, I laugh. "Well, out with it. This baby is old school. You'll need to plug in your phone to use your playlist. There's no wireless Bluetooth connection in old girls like this one."

The Buick, along with every car in Rocco's arsenal of vehicles, are jacked up with state-of-the-art equipment. I just want an excuse for Justine to whip out her phone.

Once Justine has her phone plugged in via an iPhone cable and her playlist selected, I grunt out in a long moan, "Fuck... I forgot my sunglasses. They're on the entryway table." *Where I purposely left them only minutes ago.* "Can you grab 'em for me?"

Justine glares at me like I asked her to sniff Landon's stinky socks.

"Come on, J. Walsh men aren't just hung like horses, we have big hoofers like them too. Take one for the team. I don't want to wake up Mom. Even her hungover head will hear my clumping feet a mile out."

I almost lost her with my brag, but I brought her back by reminding her how much of a light sleeper our mom is. It's a known trait of any mother, much less one with five children close in age. "Fine. But I'm getting my coat while in there."

I wait for her to curl out of the car and clamber up the front stairs before snatching her phone up from the middle console. With her belief the world isn't full of child molesters, rapists, and murderers, I unlock her phone after only two attempts of inputting the password.

Recalling Demi and Sloane's love of long chats via messenger, I log into Justine's Facebook Messenger app first. When I fail to find anything incriminating there, I move to her recently called list. My back molars smash together when I notice call after call after call the past three weeks have been from one number. She hasn't added her caller's credentials to her contact list, but I don't need to be Sherlock Holmes to discover who the number belongs to. I merely need to push a single button.

After drifting my eyes to my family home and noting Justine's shadow in the arched window on the top half of the compound, I hit the number blowing up her phone at all times or the day and night, then squash her phone to my ear.

"That was quick. I hope you're calling to accept my invitation?" greets an unfamiliar British accent at the same time Justine breathes out furiously, "What are you doing on *my* phone?"

When she snatches her phone out of my hand, my eyes snap

to the arched window she careened past only seconds ago. I realize my error when the shadow's hair swishes out from behind her back when she steps away from the window to conceal her watch. Justine's red locks are hanging over her shoulders like lava. Demi is the only one who wears her hair in a ponytail no matter the occasion.

My eyes drop back to Justine when she screams her frustration into the street before adding words into the mix. "This needs to stop, Maddox! You *all* need to stop!" Her shouted words switch on numerous lights in our family home. "I'm not a child, so why do you continually treat me as if I am one?"

Although I'd rather bookmark our conversation for a better time and location, there's no stopping it. Justine has reached the end of her tether. There are no seconds remaining on the detonator.

After joining her on the sidewalk, I say in a calm, respectable manner, "I am well aware you're not a child." The only reason I'm able to keep my cool is because the accent wasn't close to being Italian. It dropped the nerves from my stomach quicker than Landon races to the toilet after too much Mexican.

Justine whips around so fast you'd swear I told her I signed her on to become a nun during our last family meeting. Although Saint suggested it, for the most part, he was joking. *I think.* "No, you don't! *None* of you do. I'm twenty years old with *five* overbearing fathers! *Five*, Maddox! One is bad enough, but I have to put up with quintuple that!"

I hate the angst on her face, but it won't stop me from saying, "We are only like this because we care about you, J. We don't want to see you getting hurt."

I take a step back, emotionally winded when she fires back with words that maim both my heart and my soul. "So your brilliant plan to stop me from getting hurt is to *hurt* me?" She scoffs, then folds her arms under her chest. "Now I understand why you were single for so long. It wasn't because you wanted to play the field or sow your oats. It was because you think loving something gives you the right to lie to them, manipulate them, and treat them like brainless idiots!"

"You're not being fair, J. You have no fucking clue what some people in this town are capable of—"

"Because my brothers won't give me the chance to experience real life!" Justine interrupts as her eyes dart between Landon, Caidyn, and Saint now watching our interaction from the front lawn instead of the safety of their rooms. "You're suffocating me like you are suffocating Demi."

Although her claim is for all the male members of our family, I take it personally. "I'm not suffocating Demi. I am *protecting* her."

Justine locks her eyes with mine. They're full of tears, but their sheen is barely seen through her annoyance. "From what, Maddox? Me? You? *Them?*" She thrusts her hand at Landon, Caidyn, and Saint, who are hovering closer. "Who are you protecting her from?"

Ignoring Caidyn's warning for me to choose my words wisely, I step closer to Justine. "From stuff I can't tell you right now." When she blows a hot breath out of her nose, I talk faster. "Not because I don't want to tell you, J, but because it isn't my story to tell."

I'm getting through to her. Our mom often quoted professor Brené Brown during our teen years. 'We share with people who have earned the right to hear our story' is one of Justine's favorite quotes, but Landon fucks it up with his inability to understand the inner-workings of a college student. "We're not being deceitful to hurt you, Justine. Whether you believe us or not doesn't alter the facts. We're doing this for your own good."

With her attitude at its peak, Justine angles her head to the side before arching a brow. "So you admit you are *lying* to me?"

Landon blubbers out a string of indecipherable words, briskly shakes his head, then blurts out, "That wasn't what I meant."

"Lying and being deceitful are the same thing, Landon." When none of her brothers jump in to back up her claims, Justine balls her hands into tiny fists, silently squeals, then she spins on her heels and walks in the opposite direction.

I clear the angst from my voice to ensure I don't say something I can't take back before asking, "Where are you going, J?"

Although she cranks her head my way, she continues walking. "Back to school, where I plan to stay until you all start telling the truth."

"Justine."

When Landon's growly warning doesn't slow her strides, Caidyn gives empathy a try. "I understand your frustration, Justine, but walking away won't solve anything. We're family. We stick together."

She throws open the door of her beat-up Honda like Caidyn never spoke, then slips behind the steering wheel.

Saint gets slapped in the chest by Caidyn, and Landon hits him with a stern finger point when he mutters, "You're acting like a spoiled brat."

"Good," Justine finally responds. "It's about time one of your annoying traits rubbed off on me." Her narrowed eyes expose her reply isn't solely for Saint. We're all on her shitlist—even me. Her favorite.

"Let her go," I say to Caidyn when the abrupt closure of Justine's door replicates a rocket being rammed up his ass. He's seconds from takeoff. "I'll talk to her once she has calmed down."

Even with his concerned gaze focused on Justine, Caidyn's words are for me. "You said it yourself, Maddox. This isn't your story to tell."

"Then I'll talk to her," offers a much more feminine voice. After stopping at my side, Demi slips her clammy hand into mine. "She might understand your objectives if it comes directly from the source of your worry."

"Dem—"

"It's fine, Maddox."

I wait for her to tack on the two words that always announce she's far from fine. When that doesn't happen, I rub my thumb over the veins pulsating in her hand. "You don't have to do this. I'd rather wrangle a temperamental sister than force the woman I love to relive her nightmares."

As her lips curve into a smile, her eyes go misty. "When you say it like that, how could I renege my offer?" Even with my brothers eyeballing our exchange like perverts, the sexual chemistry between us is palpable. "But I would like to talk to her in person. I don't want to consider what my uncle would do if he hears I shared guarded family secrets. If there's no evidence, you can't prosecute, right?"

Her soundless gag when she mentions her uncle hides the panic I see in her eyes. Col has been out of town for almost two months, yet Demi continually peers over her shoulder. It's a habit I'd give anything to change but fully comprehend. It is easy to tell someone to look ahead when they haven't faced evil head-on.

"I agree, you should talk in person. Everything is better in the flesh." I catch her off guard by pulling her toward me with a gentle tug on her wrist before banding an arm around her thighs and tossing her onto my shoulder. "So while we give Justine a couple of minutes to calm down, how about I show you not all secrets are bad?"

When I swat her backside, I hear Demi's smile in her scorn. "I haven't brushed my hair or my teeth! I'm still in my pajamas, for crying out loud." She waits for me to place her into the passenger seat Justine's backside heated for all of two seconds before she lifts her eyes to mine. "Can I at least get changed?"

"Nope. Clothes aren't necessary where we're going."

Her voice is a cross between turned on and confused when she whispers my name in a husky tone. "Maddox—"

I cut off any objection she's planning to give by buckling her in, closing her door, then jogging around to the open driver's side door. I have one foot in the Buick's cab when the reason for the swift change up smacks into me.

Caidyn jerks up his chin when I ask him to forward me Justine's school schedule. His response when I request for him to do it anywhere but at the Walsh family cabin is nowhere near as polite, but since I'm a hothead who rarely follows the playbook, I act as if he gives me the go-ahead.

Caidyn won't care. He was raised in the same household as me, so he's well aware the Walsh brethren don't follow a rule book. We lead with our hearts while praying like fuck our heads get us out of the trouble love made us blind to.

If forced between taking a risk or losing the chance, I almost always choose the former, but when it comes to Demi, there's no question. She is a risk I will always take.

1 2

DEMI

I eye Maddox curiously when he requests I close my eyes. I know the street he's turned down. We've driven this very road multiple times the past couple of weeks, so why do I need to close my eyes?

With a chuckle that announces he loves my newfound stubbornness, Maddox tosses a pair of knee-high socks to my side of the car. "I'll never force you to do anything you don't want to do… *but*… you're doing this."

"I am *not* putting your smelly gym socks anywhere near my face."

We've been together almost twenty-four seven the past two months, but the jealousy in my reply can't be helped. The couple of weeks Maddox courted Harlow Murphy her senior year was the longest relationship he had during our teen years. Its shortness didn't make the hurt any less, though. I swear I was the only person on this side of the continent who cheered when they broke up, and even then, my win didn't feel that victorious when rumors circulated about the reason for their breakup.

I'm glad not every woman in my hometown faced the childhood I did, but I still thought they'd need more than a stinky sock phobia to leave. Women and children are abused daily in my uncle's industry, yet they're forced to stay.

My eyes lift from my balled hands into my lap to Maddox when he says, "For one, they're not my socks. They are yours." I twist my lips. *I thought they looked familiar.* "Two, Harlow and I didn't break up because my gym socks fucking reek." He takes a second to relish my stunned expression before pushing out with a smile, "And three, you're as cute as fuck when you are jealous."

"I'm not jealous." *I am, but I'm not saying anything that will double the pompous gleam in his eyes.* "I'm just…" Of all the days words could fail me, it happens to be today. "You seemed close… *kind of in love.*" My last four words are mumbles.

I choke on my spit when Maddox replies nonchalantly, "We were." He grins like I'm not seconds from extraditing myself from his car by rolling onto the asphalt. "But it was like the love I have for my sister. There were no fireworks or moral-blinding chemistry. We gelled. It was simply more friendship-based instead of the rock-solid shit that will bind me to you for eternity."

Through a gag, I ask, "How are you not working for Hallmark?" I sound upset even though I'm far from it.

I understand what Maddox is saying. It was the same for me when I accepted dates during our final year of high school. I didn't want to be schmoozed. I simply didn't want to be alone. My family is massive and spans across many continents, but I was so far from anyone's thoughts, I was truly an outcast.

That's why I so desperately craved to become a Walsh.

In a way, I have become one the last couple of weeks. It's better than I could have ever imagined.

With that in mind, I unkink the knot in the knee-high socks, slip one over my eyes, then secure it behind the back of my head.

"Can you see anything?"

Excluding the scratchy white material making me excessively blink, I can't see a thing. Although I am confident in saying Maddox is waving his hand in front of my face. I can't see shadows, but the movement of his arm whips up his yummy scent. It makes me even hungrier than the grumble of my stomach announcing we haven't had breakfast.

"Maddox," I push out with a moan when he brushes the back of his hand down my budded nipple.

I lose the chance to shamefully beg for him to do it again when the noise of gravel under tires almost drowns out his reply, "What? I had to check you couldn't see. You're a snoop."

"Since when has a boob-grab helped with eyesight?"

I can't see Maddox, but the heat of his smile is undeniable. "Technically, they don't. But…" He leaves me hanging long enough for sweat to bead on the top of my brow. "If your wickedly deviant head had spotted my hand's approach, you would have pushed out your chest in silent pleading for me to hurry. The fact it stayed still, exposed you can't see shit." The aimless wave of my hand smacks into his rock-hard midsection a mere second before he raises it to his mouth to kiss the edge. He grazes his teeth over the meaty flesh, places a second kiss on the inside of my hand, then sets it back onto my lap. "Wait for me to come get you."

When I lift my chin in understanding, he pops open the driver's side door and steps out onto the gravel driveway of the Walsh family cabin. With one of my senses down, the other one takes up the slack. I hear him climb the front stairs of the porch and drag something across the lacquered wood before a crumbling noise overtakes the gentle splashes of water on the rocks behind me.

A bundle of nerves takes flight in my stomach when the distinctive stomp of Maddox's feet drowns out the frantic beat of my heart. Excluding my twenty-second birthday, I've never been given a surprise before—well, not a good one.

Cool winds whip up around my legs when Maddox opens my door. They do little to dampen the fire roaring inside of me when my hunt for his lips from him leaning across me to undo my seat belt comes up trumps. The scruff on his chin keeps my accuracy high. It's wiry but devastating to my senses when he uses it against me in the bedroom. It doesn't matter where we are or what we are doing, the quickest whiff of his facial hair sends my head into a tailspin. It conjures up memories of long lovemaking sessions, greedy fucks, and the heart-mending snuggles we do after every marathon romp.

Maddox Walsh is a beautiful canvas, but his insides are the real artwork.

"My mom always said my mouth would get me in trouble," Maddox murmurs over my mouth after showing his appreciation for my inability to keep my hands to myself. "If I had any clue this was what she meant, I would have done it sooner." I wish like hell for the sock to slip off my face when he drags the tip of his finger down my nose. His eyes are always the bluest when he does that. It is as if it calms him as much as it does me. "Watch your head as you come out. Caidyn will kill me if a drop of your blood spills here."

He uses Caidyn as his scapegoat anytime he feels out of his comfort zone. He thinks he doesn't have what it takes to pull off Caidyn's suaveness. I'm not so inclined to agree.

"Two more steps, then we're heading right."

"Right?" I ask, certain I heard him wrong. Nothing but a small patch of grass is on the right. Mr. Walsh has stated numerous times he didn't buy this plot of land for its size and accessibility. It was the views he was sold on. Almost every window in the cabin has a water view because Mrs. Walsh designed it that way.

Instead of answering me, Maddox guides me to the far end of the front porch. How do I know we're at the end if I can't see? The sun that's slowly rising is beaming through the threads of the sock.

"Stay right there." Maddox waits for me to nod before he shuffles away from me. When he speaks again, he only sounds around three or four feet away from me. "On the count of three, remove your blindfold—"

"On three or after three?"

He chuckles about my need to know everything down to the finest detail before he commences counting down. "One... two... three!"

I yank off my blindfold with so much excitement, the time I was almost choked by one is pushed to the back of my mind.

My excitement doesn't blister for long.

"What is it?" I ask Maddox, who's standing next to a pile of wood palings with his arms held out like he's a model on *The Price is Right!*

I don't know whether to burst out laughing or crying when he replies, "It's a doghouse." He rakes his eyes over the mismatched wood pieces before mumbling, "Well, it *will* be a doghouse… when I finish building it."

"You're building a doghouse?" My voice is so high, it sounds as if I sucked on helium.

When Maddox nods, I question sheepishly, "For me?" Tears prick my eyes when he nods his head for the second time. "You're getting me a dog?"

When Sloane forced me to write a wish list for my eighteenth birthday, I only jotted down three things. For my dad to still be here, to be free of this life, and to have a dog. I then burned the letter in the fireplace at Sloane's demand and shut down any hope of my guardian angel granting me my wishes. Maddox can't bring back my dad, but every day I spend with him makes the loss more bearable.

"I'm not getting you a dog, Demi." Maddox speaks as if he doesn't know the dams in my eyes are about to spill over. "*I'm* building you a doghouse. *You're* buying the dog. Then we'll live together, happily ever after." He traces the slither of silver in my right cheek before murmuring words I've heard him mumble many times the past few weeks. "You're strong enough to stand by yourself, but I'd rather you didn't need to."

His mumbled words shift to a moan when I balance on my tippytoes so I can plant my lips on his mouth. Words can't express how happy he makes me, and I much prefer showing him.

Lust consumes me when Maddox takes control of our kiss.

It's a deep, warm, carnal embrace, but the initial reservedness of his kiss catches me off guard. We're normally clawing at each other by the second duel of our tongues, panting with want and shameless to where we are when the urge to maul each other hits.

This morning's kiss is far from savage. It's tender, loving, and sickly sweet, and it has me craving so much more.

"Not yet," Maddox murmurs against my skin when he drops his lips from my mouth to my neck. "If we start this now, the doghouse will never be built."

I've never been more torn in my life. I have wanted a dog almost all my life, something I could love as my own, but I've also wanted Maddox just as long.

When I say that to Maddox, he mutters, "Fuck, Demi. You can't say shit like that to me and expect me to act like a gentleman. I'm trying to schmooze you, treat you how you deserve to be treated, but now all I'm thinking about is fucking you on a pile of wood, hopeful a splinter in the ass will remind me that today is meant to be about your dreams, not mine."

I step closer to him, grinning like a cat eyeing a bowl of milk when my closeness doubles the thickness behind the zipper in his trousers. "Why can't it be about *our* dreams?"

"You know I can't multitask. I'm not cut out for that shit. It will start out being about you, then it will shift to me and my greedy cock. It has no class when it comes to you."

I breathe in the moan he releases when I scrub my hand over the bulge in his pants. "Good. I very much like it that way."

"Demi…" His groan makes it seem as if I'm truly killing him, and it has me switching tactics in an instant. "Fine. We will do it your way." I gallop down the two stairs that lead to the microscopic patch of grass like my thoughts aren't as sinister as they are. "Did this come with instructions, or are we going in blind?"

"That's it?" Maddox's tone is high enough to cause an echo. "You're going to tease me, then leave me hanging. Not cool, Demi. *Not cool.*" He playfully *tsks* me before joining me next to a pile of wood that now seems so much more sentimental. "You do realize erections don't occur by magic. Every one of them puts my heart in grave danger."

I cock my hip before splaying my hands across it. "Really? I thought I just needed to breathe in your direction to make you hard enough to drill for gold."

Maddox cusses under his breath when I add evidence to my claim by circling my lips and blowing air in his direction. "For you, that's how it works, but it wasn't always like that."

The lust roaring through my veins switches out for hot, potent jealousy.

It dawns on me that we both have skeletons in our closet when Maddox mumbles, "Now I know why Flint made a mess in his pants. He didn't just get an up-close and personal view of your lips, he got to taste them too."

"Once," I remind him, my voice surprisingly strong for how heavy the tension is between us. "You'll get them for a lifetime."

There's nothing soft about our kiss this time around. It's savage and unhinged. Claiming and full of need. An explosion of tongues, wandering hands, and unvoiced promises. We attack each other without burden, aware we're both where we are meant to be even with us being in full view of the neighbors.

"Lean back against the cladding of the cabin. You'll be out of sight there," Maddox says a couple of minutes later, his voice breathless and husky from our kiss.

When I do as requested, his eyes study me. They rake up my body, soaking in every inch until the chemistry bristling between us hisses and cracks.

"I should carry you inside, cherish you on my bed like I did your first night here…" He pauses, draws his brows together, then corrects, "You're *only* night here. But I can't. The view is too fucking spectacular to alter… the sun's hues bouncing off your skin, the sexy rise and fall of your chest as you contemplate us getting busted, and the fact you also believe we are where we're meant to be. It's untouchable. Faultless. Way too fucking perfect." I nod. He doesn't need my agreement, he can see it in my eyes, but it felt nice expressing it. "If only we had time."

"There's always time to put important things first. You're important, Maddox…" I settle the nerves in my throat before adding, "And so am I."

If you exclude the searing admiration beaming out of him, the expression on his face mimics the one it had when I took up his offer to play with his 'gun' at the range weeks ago. "You are, and I'm so fucking glad you're starting to realize that."

We get lost in one another for the next several minutes. Maddox strives to push his kissing skillset from a ten out of ten to an eleven while I do my best to show him how much I appreciate him teaching me that I deserve better. I've often said I'm a little naïve on aspects of my family's businesses. In reality, I *acted* naïve because I believed it was the only way I could keep those I cared about safe.

That stops now.

Letting the bullies win isn't fighting for what you believe in. It's the coward's way out.

"I love you, Maddox." I breathe out with a moan when I come up for air. "So much, sometimes it's hard to breathe when your lips aren't on mine."

He says he loves me back before he tells me he'd move mountains to ensure I'm never without his lips. "Nothing will come between us, Demi. Not a mountain, a river, or another continent. We will always be together."

When he brushes the back of his hand against my panties to test how wet his promise made me, I peel them off my dripping pussy and down my legs before I stuff them into the pocket of his trousers. We're acting like two horny teenagers at a prom, but I adore every single moment of our step back in time.

Although I did attend prom, it came at a cost. Entering a packed room with the eyes of hundreds of students on you is daunting enough, let alone facing a second gauntlet only hours later with men more than double your age.

My uncle didn't believe I was thankful for the dress he had purchased for me. Instead of accepting my offer to pay him back by working at Petretti's free of charge, he devised his own punishment.

It was then that I realized how horrendous his crimes were. He had buyers at the ready in under an hour and bids from as far as Japan. I was all but sold, my stay of execution only granted when I fell to his knees and begged.

A night that should have ranked high when I looked back on my memories soon became a nightmare. It was the first time my uncle's comments were inappropriate for someone who shares his blood. His constant references about my virginity made me extremely uncomfortable, so I won't mention how sick I felt when he hinted that it would be a good gift to give someone to show my thanks for their 'years of gallant support.'

When he left me alone to consider suitable candidates, I did the complete opposite. I made a beeline for the weakest man in his crew who also had the biggest mouth.

The sex was meaningless. There were no emotions attached to it whatsoever, but it was via my choice, and any guilt I felt for not saving myself for 'the one' was forgotten when news reached my uncle's ears. That was the first time he slapped me in front of an audience, but the words he shouted while humiliating me in front of his associates were priceless. "Get out of my face! I never want to see you again."

Those three short weeks he 'abandoned' me were precious. I moved in with Sloane, got a job at a family-run pizzeria, and slept most nights with the lights off.

It all came crumbling down when I arrived for my third Friday night shift. The seats in the pizzeria weren't filled with hungry patrons. There wasn't a slice of pizza or pitcher of beer to be seen in any of the black trench-coat donned customers' hands. My uncle was back to his old tricks, but I was old enough not to fall for them.

Well, so I thought.

Family-minded people don't like dining in the same establishments as mafia men. Within a week, regulars stopped coming to Donny's. Within a month, the phone number associated with his delivery service stopped ringing. Donny was weeks away from bankruptcy.

I couldn't let that happen, so just like my uncle, I fell back to my old tricks.

I begged.

On the condition I got to live in my own apartment, Donny got to keep his pizzeria, and I would repay my debt to my uncle by recruiting fighters for his underground fight syndicate.

Easy enough, right?

Wrong.

The very first name on the top of the stack was Saint Walsh.

Maddox's was a very close second.

For months, I stupidly recruited the best fighters I stumbled across who had no association to the Walsh brethren, all the while making out to my uncle that I was close to signing his unicorn fighters.

You know the rest of the story from there. It has both good and bad parts.

When an unexpected tremor darts down my spine, Maddox murmurs against my neck, "If you want me to stop, Demi, tell me to stop. I'll stop before the 's' leaves your mouth."

We've had many discussions that newly fledging couples shouldn't have the past two months, but the circumstances surrounding the loss of my virginity haven't been widely examined. Maddox knows it was via my choice, but his constant reminders that I never have to do anything I don't want has me wary if he's held similar talks with other people.

The man I gave my virginity to is no longer a part of my uncle's crew, but news about what we had done circulated amongst the men even faster than the confusion as to why my uncle was so upset.

Hating that I'm letting memories of my past sully new memories, I pop open the button of Maddox's trousers before lowering the zipper.

"Hold up," Maddox says, placing his hand over mine. "What's going on in that head of yours. You've got a big ol' crinkle right here." He rubs his thumb down the middle of my forehead. "You only ever get a groove there when you're fretting."

"I'm not fretting. I'm fine." I inwardly curse before trying to pull the wool over his eyes for the second time. "I'm just tired. We had an early start after a late night. I'm wrecked."

"Nope."

That's it.

That's *all* he says.

Nope.

"I'm afraid we will be seen." I'm not proud of my ability to lie without flinching, but when the odds are stacked against you, you have to give it your best shot.

Maddox denies my lie with a shake of his head this time around. "Try again." When my lips twitch, he adds, "And give honesty a shot this time. Lying doesn't suit you."

The disappointment in his tone is like a knife to the chest. "It's my uncle." The fact his facial expression doesn't alter advises he was aware of who my unease centers around. "Something feels off. Don't get me wrong, I'm glad he's gone, but I'm just shocked he gave up so easily."

My once-inflated chest deflates even more when Maddox places me back onto my feet. "Saint said the same thing. Col is the king, and Dimitri is the prince, so why is Dimitri the one giving orders?"

I shrug, truly confused. "It was most certainly *not* like that two years ago."

Hearing something in my voice I didn't mean to express,

Maddox asks, "Do you think the change-up has something to do with Dimitri's daughter? She'd be around that age."

"Fien is two?" My cousin's unknown daughter was one of the many discussions we've had the past couple of weeks.

Maddox rakes his fingers through his hair before lifting his chin. "Two-ish? It's hard to tell from a photo."

"At least he has a photo. All I remember of Kaylee are the blurred images in my head. I can't even remember what color her eyes were."

He sucks in my sharp exhale before asking, "Are you sure you don't want me to ask Dimitri about her? He's older than you, he may remember."

Just offering to place himself on Dimitri's radar for me has me loving him even more, but I'd rather keep him as far away from my family as possible. "Dr. Avery is convinced my memories will eventually unlock. I merely need to be patient."

I pop my elbow into Maddox's rib when he mumbles, "Better you than me. I wouldn't last a week."

"I don't know about that. You did good keeping this a secret." I step past him before waving my hand over the unconstructed doghouse. "How long have you been working on it?"

"Are we talking total hours combined or straight-up days?"

I smile at the nervousness in his tone before replying, "Whatever you feel comfortable with."

He nervously shuffles foot to foot before he blurts out, "Three full days if you combined the total number of hours I've put in."

"Three days!" I whine like a child when my shout ensures any attempts to reignite the spark between Maddox and me will be nonexistent. More than a rapidly rising sun is being pointed our way, and not one of the rays is au naturel. "I know you're still striving to work out what you want to do once your studies are over, but can I suggest taking building, architecture, and any other manual labor position that requires your hands *off* your list of possible careers. If you were Noah and the doghouse was an ark, we would have drowned by now."

"Ouch…" Maddox says while clutching his chest like he's mortally wounded. "Kick a man while he's down, why don't you." When I peer at him, confused as to how he's down for the count, he nudges his head to the blindingly obvious bulge behind the zipper in his pants. "You never, I repeat, *never* diss a man's capabilities with his hands while *all* the blood in his body is feeding his cock. You could cause him *permanent* damage."

The boy I had a crush on for years shines bright in his eyes when he mutters, "There's only one way to fix the grave injustice." He nudges his head to the ground at his feet like he can't feel the eyes of at least four people on us. "On your knees, Demi…" The hot, sticky slickness his sexy voice caused between my legs dries when he finalizes his sentence. "This jigsaw puzzle isn't going to fix itself."

13

MADDOX

"Are you sure that's the one you want?"

Demi drifts her eyes away from a semi-grown Doberman cozying up to her from his cage to me. "Yes, he's perfect."

She purrs her reply in the same manner she did while taking my dick between her lips. We built the doghouse I had purchased three weeks ago, painted it a bright, sunny yellow, then got lost in each other for the spare hour we had before our appointment at an animal shelter in Ravenshoe.

Even if I hadn't stalked Demi from afar a majority of my life, I still would know she'd rather a rescue dog than a bred-to-specification puppy. There's an immense amount of pleasure in taking someone out of a volatile situation and showing them what real love means.

Love doesn't come with stipulations.

Demi is slowly learning that.

"All right, I'll let the staff know…" My words trail off when the lady I made the appointment with earlier this week arrives at our side.

Although she's a bundle of happiness, her words are far from it. "I'm sorry, I forgot to tell you, the dogs in this section of the shelter are not available for adoption." She holds a clipboard brimming with adoption papers up to her mouth so the Doberman Demi has selected won't hear her. "He's scheduled to be euthanized this afternoon."

"Why?" Demi asks after standing to her feet. "If we want to adopt him, why does he have to be put down?"

Illa, the clerk at the animal shelter, drops her lower lip into a pout. "Because he has been deemed menacing. He bit one of the staff. He needed ten stitches."

I stray my eyes to the dog she's calling a menace, confident she has her files mixed up. He spent the past twenty minutes licking Demi like she is a lollipop. He's a gentle giant. "Are you sure that dog bit someone? He's harmless."

Demi backs up my claims by squatting back down to the dog's level. "He just needs some TLC, don't you, buddy?" He leans into her embrace when she scratches under his chin, but I do notice his docked tail remains perfectly still. Demi is right. He wants affection, he just has no clue how to respond to it since he's never been given it.

"We'll take him."

"Sir—"

"I'll sign anything necessary. Indemnity forms. A statutory declaration saying you cautioned us against him. Anything you want for *that* dog." I'd offer her every dollar hidden in my childhood bedroom at my family home if it guarantees she'll give Demi the dog she wants. That's how much I'm moved by the love beaming out of Demi's eyes. I'll steal the damn dog if I have to. "Please," I shamefully beg when I appear to be getting through to her. "He just needs a little bit of love."

After taking in the dog playfully licking Demi's cheek, she releases a heavy sigh. "It will take hours in paperwork."

I mentally fist pump the air before saying coolly, "That's fine."

"And you'll need to register him at the council as a menacing dog. That alone will require an approved area for him to be housed, an additional payment for insurance, and they may even request for him to attend obedience school."

"Still fine."

A cash register's *cha-ching* sounds on repeat in my ears, but it's barely audible over the spike in my pulse when Demi throws her arms around my neck and whispers in my ear, "Thank you! He's perfect."

One hour and twenty-seven minutes later, we leave the shelter as brand-new parents of an eight-month-old Doberman named Max. Although he shook like he was thrown into an ice bath when Demi entered his stall to put on his lead, he followed her out of the shelter. He even did the occasional twirl when we broke into the parking lot. He knew his days were numbered, so he knows precisely who to thank for his second chance.

"How could they have ever called you menacing?" Demi says

to Max as she opens the back-passenger door of the Buick to place him in with his new doggy seat belt.

I laugh when Max's dive into the Buick is quickly chased by him leaping over the seat so that he sits in the front passenger seat. "Come on, buddy, in the back."

I freeze partway to the Buick when Max bares his teeth at me. He isn't growling, but I'm reasonably sure he'll gnaw my nuts off if I move one step closer.

"Front seat it is."

While struggling to conceal her smug grin, Demi latches Max into place before sliding into the back seat behind him. I stomp to the driver's seat, wordlessly announcing my annoyance that my hand can't warm Demi's thigh during our drive.

It's my favorite thing to do, and Max just stole it from me.

"Holy Mother of God." I squeal like a bitch when my slide into the driver's seat has my ear almost chewed off by a vicious, wild beast. Max is up in my face, growling, seething, and barking like a police attack dog.

I fall out of the car before my face is ripped off. Mercifully, Demi does the same, but her maneuver is more eloquent than mine. She lands on her feet, and I kick up dust with my ass.

"What the hell was that?" Demi asks after joining me at the front of the Buick's hood. Her voice is as high as my brows. I'm as shocked as hell by the seemingly placid puppy sitting in the passenger seat of Rocco's Buick, giving Demi gaga eyes. That was *not* the face seething an inch from mine only moments ago. "It's like a switch inside of him flicked on when you got in the car."

"It was more than a switch. He's a fucking psycho. We need to ask for a refund."

Demi stops my stomp back to the animal shelter by bracing her hand on my arm. "Let me try something?"

"Oh, hell no," I push out when she finalizes her sentence by slowly pacing toward the open driver's side door.

I step back with my hands held in the air when Max responds to my grab of Demi's arm by fogging the windshield with a string of growls. He's fastened in, so technically, I should feel safe. I just don't.

"Demi, if you get in that car…" I hate threatening her. It is the bane of my existence, and my objectives haven't changed because we adopted a schizophrenic dog, but I don't have a choice. She could get hurt. That overtakes anything. Morals. Ethics. Integrity. None of that matters when her life is on the line. "I'll… I'll…" I can't do it. I can't threaten her. So instead, I support her as I promised the night she cried in my arms. "Please be careful."

After jerking up her chin, she rounds the car door. "Hey, Maxie. What's got you all worked up?" The licking of Max's lips is for Demi, but his evil glare is solely devoted to me. "I know he looks big and burly, but he really is a softie." Aware her comment was for me, I roll my eyes. She often jokes I've been able to grow a beard since I was fourteen so I could easily slot into the big 'teddy' genre. "He just wants to get you out of here as fast as me."

I don't breathe when she slots into the driver's seat, then I hit Max with a stern glare when he fails to cite an objection to her intrusion. I can't say I blame him. If I had to pick between sitting next to Demi or me, I'd always choose the former.

"Come on," Demi says with a giggle a short time later, loving the jealousy on my face. "If you behave, maybe he'll let you have the front seat next time."

With a grumble like she reneged on an offer of a blowjob on the way home, I trudge my way to the seat Max should be sitting in, for once, bowing out of a fight without any bloodshed.

MADDOX

"Sweet mother of Jesus, we were playing, you friggin' lunatic!" The pure bliss on Demi's face switches to worry when I stumble back with a grumble. "Max needs to learn the difference between your moans and groans. He bit me on the ass." I angle my head to the side when Demi clamps a hand over her mouth to stifle her giggles. "It isn't funny. I think he drew blood." She laughs even louder when I attempt to assess the damage Max did. Years of fighting have made me flexible both on and off the canvas, but not even rubber limbs would have me authenticating his bite is as vicious as his bark. "He's not even sorry. Look at him." I nudge my head to Max sitting next to our bed, grinning with his eyes. "He's fucking smiling."

"Aww. He is smiling. Look at that adorable face." I pout like a child when Demi scoots across the mattress so she can scratch Max under his sloppy jowls. He drools as much as Demi does when she's sleeping. He just does it while he's awake. Excessive fluctuance seems to be his ultimate nighttime trick.

When I say that to Demi, she playfully tosses her fist into my stomach. It doubles Max's toothy grin. "Don't be a sourpuss. This was *your* plan. You wanted me to have a guard dog."

"Yeah, I did," I confess, unable to lie. "But I wanted him to keep *other* men away from you. Not me. I've barely sampled your lips the past two days. Killjoy over here..." I once again nudge my head to a three-foot brick shithouse with fur, "... loves ruining my fun."

My point is proven without precedent when Demi endeavors to lift my dropping lip by pressing her mouth to mine. I barely get in one full lick before Max is up in my business, warning me to back the fuck off without nothing but a glare.

"Your dog hates me."

"He doesn't hate you," Demi talks over my mouth. She's so desperate to have my lips on her, she's willing to place my ass on the line to get it.

I'm not as eager. Max eats more than Caidyn and me combined, but I swear he eyes my cock like its sausage meat hanging in a deli window every single time I exit the bathroom in the buff. "He hates me enough, I'm confident in saying he'd rip my dick off without hesitation if he knew you wouldn't be upset." When I hit Demi with a flirty wink, my cock twitches back to life. "Lucky that will *never* occur within the next million years."

My jaw falls to the floor when Demi shrugs. "It's all right, but a million years is pushing it."

"*All right?* You think my cock is only *all right*?" I clutch my chest, certain I'm about to die. "How could you be so cruel. What did my cock ever do to you?"

I get where Demi is going with this when she mutters, "The past two days... *not a damn thing.*" She returns my frisky wink, toothy grin and all. "Why do you think I'm trying to goad him into proving his *abilities*." She says 'abilities' with a purr that could have me doing a Flint. My cock hardens in an instant, and even quicker than that, I've forgotten about the fanged mental patient standing guard next to his owner.

After playfully tackling her, I pin Demi to our bed, uncaring that she's freshly showered and smelling divine, whereas I reek to high heaven from an hour workout in the gym after my last run. My fight last Friday almost saw Dimitri's investment take a loss. If Demi hadn't shouted out my opponent's weak spot I missed during our seven-round bout, I would have come out of the match a loser, and a majority of that loss could be blamed on me not putting in the hours of a full-time fighter. Well, if you exclude my part-time career as a drug mule.

Ignoring the bitter taste in the back of my mouth, I drag my scratchy beard down Demi's stomach. The roughness of my beard near the apex of her thighs immediately suspends the scissor-like movements of her legs. She freezes like she did when I first found her in a towel before her hands fist the blanket and her eyes locked on me.

I'm about to slice my tongue through the scent keeping my dick rock hard when Max responds exactly as he did only minutes ago. He bites me right on the ass, except this time, he aims a little bit lower, bringing his maiming fangs to within an inch of my nut sack.

"Fuck that. I'm out." I dive off the bed with my hands held in the air and a throbbing backside.

Demi's giggles are replaced with a groan when I bend down to gather my sweatpants off the floor. The image of Demi splayed before me in nothing but a teeny tiny very teasing nightie has my blood at boiling point, but I'd rather sweat like a man in a sauna than have my nuts eaten by a vicious Doberman.

"You're bleeding." Max's upturned lips sag when Demi shifts her narrowed eyes to him. "Max…" She could say more, but she doesn't need to. Max's foaming jowls landing on the carpet expose he understands her disappointment. He isn't upset that he hurt me. He just loathes disappointing Demi. "Stay here." After using the signal she learned on a YouTube tutorial, Demi slips off the bed and joins me at the end. "Come on, I have anti-septic ointment in the bathroom." When I pull a face, she adds, "Don't act like you didn't know this would eventually happen. Even I've occasionally thought about sinking my teeth into your ass." She rakes her teeth over her bottom lip in a sexy, cock-thickening way. "It's too perfect not to want a little nibble."

With a grin of a smug prick, I follow her into the bathroom, closing the door behind me. After checking the door's sturdi-ness, ensuring it can withstand the brutal charge of a Dober-man, I spin around to face Demi. My pout matches Max's when I spot a cotton ball soaked in iodine in her hand. I thought her helpful nurse ruse was a ploy to get us alone without her attack dog at her side. I'm not sure if I should be disappointed or swoon that she wants to take care of me, so I do both.

"When was your last tetanus shot?"

Demi's pretty blue eyes float up to mine. "Mine?" When I nod my head, she twists her lips. "I think I had a booster when I was around fourteen or so. Why? I don't see Max ever biting me."

"I wasn't asking for you." Her dark brows pull together in confusion. I attempt to alleviate it by saying, "I was asking for me. If you're vaccinated, there'll be less chance of me getting a tetanus infection if you bite my ass while tending to my 'wound.'" I air quote my last word like she's using Max's bite as an excuse to ogle my assets.

Her smile could bring any man to his knees. I always said her smiles are my favorite, and nothing has changed in the past two months. "Bend over the tub, *Dick* Walsh. Ass high in the air."

I strut across the room. Yeah, I said strut. Even my dick swings with each step I take. That's how cocky the sexual chemistry that forever surges between Demi and me makes me.

Some of my peacock feathers bend when Demi doubles my arch over the bathtub by pushing down on my lower back. If I didn't know any better, I'd swear she's prepping me for a prostate exam.

I'm convinced she can read minds when the clench of my ass cheeks causes her breathy chuckles to condensate on my butt cheeks. The tiny beads of moisture shred the last of my composure. My ass is aching, and I'm reasonably sure I can smell Max standing behind the door, but I can't have my girl this close to my cock and act nonchalant.

That's above my paygrade.

Out of my league.

He-Man wouldn't be strong enough to endure this, so I don't stand a fucking chance.

I almost whine when Demi foils my endeavor to poke her in the eye with my dick by standing and moving back to the vanity. "You may need a tetanus shot." She dumps the cotton ball she used to clean my wound into the bin before spinning around to face me. "He dug his teeth in pretty deep…" Her words trail off when her eyes trek of my body lands on my dick. "Sweet Lord."

I take a moment to savor the press of her thighs before lifting my chin, wordlessly demanding for her to bring her sweetness to me. My head slants when she shakes her head for the quickest second. She isn't denying me. She's evening the score, making us equal. She wants me to prove I want her as much as she wants me, and that she doesn't always need to give first to receive back. She can be prioritized first.

"Always," I murmur like she can hear my thoughts. "Don't ever forget that, Demi."

She watches me cross the room, ignorant to the scratches Max is inflicting on the wooden door with his claws. At this moment in time, there's no one in the world but me, which means she's safe, protected, and very much loved. I'd never let anything happen to her.

I breathe in the air she releases from me weaving my fingers through her long locks so I can tug her head back. She's been wearing her hair down more often lately. I'm unsure if that's because she's finally learned not everyone will use it against her or because Max is as jealous of her scrunchies as he is of me getting close to Demi. He tugs them out of Demi's hair more often than I do.

I wait until Demi is on the verge of begging before locking our lips. Even after all this time, I still need to know she is here because she wants to be.

As the smell I'm obsessed with doubles in intensity, I slide my tongue between Demi's parted lips before dueling it with hers. While fucking her mouth with my tongue, I slide my hand up one of her thighs, hissing into her mouth when the heat of her pussy scorches my hand. She's on fucking fire.

"Please," Demi begs on a moan when the needs of her pussy become too much to bear. She's grinding down on my hand, taking what she needs, but she still needs more.

After lifting her to sit on the vanity, I tug her forward until her pussy hangs off the marble countertop, then fall to my knees. Demi doesn't cite an objection to the changeup. Her eyes twinkle with desire as a ghost-like smile curls her lips. She thinks I'm obsessed with eating her pussy because I want her to feel superior. In reality, I'm obsessed with how good she tastes. I'd keep her pussy on my mouth for eternity if I could.

"Lean back a bit. Bring that sweet pussy to my mouth." Forever trusting, Demi does as requested without the slightest bit of hesitation. "Now watch me. Everything is better when it's witnessed firsthand."

After grinding the tip of my nose over the nervy bud between her legs, I spear my tongue inside of her. She bucks out immediately, the sensation of two days of prolonged foreplay heightening her senses.

She's so fucking sensitive, her thighs hug my head before I've notched half a finger inside of her. I pump in and out of her slickened pussy on repeat while hitting her clit with rapid-fired flicks of my tongue.

The more Demi moans, the louder Max barks. He's scratching at the door so crazily, I'm beginning to wonder if his claws are axes.

Aware not even a third bite to the ass will stop me from making Demi come, I eat her more expertly. I push my tongue inside of her, lapping up the goodness my fingers caused before moving my slicked fingers to her clit. I fuck her with my tongue, stimulate her clit with my fingers, then speak a heap of the dirty words that make her shatter like glass on a concrete floor.

As a simpering growl rumbles in Demi's chest, I mutter against the lips of her pussy, "Do it. Come on my face. Give me that sweetness."

I smile about the cute noises she releases when she comes before attempting to stretch her orgasm from one to two. The room spins when the sweet flavors of her orgasm coat my tongue. She tastes so good. It's an addictive, extravagant banquet I lap up like a dog on heat.

"Oh, God… I can't… it's too much," Demi pushes out between big breaths a couple of seconds later. She's shuddering so much the brutal shake of her thighs is heard in her voice. "I need a minute… just one."

I do one big lick up her slit to curb my desires for an hour or two before standing to my feet. I've barely dragged the back of my hand over my wet lips when Demi spots the thickness her taste always causes to my cock. She mutters, "Fuck sanity. I'd rather die than give this up," under her breath before she shoves me back with more force than a woman her size should have.

The bathtub jabbing into the back of my knees folds them, then Demi aids in my fall by pushing down on my shoulders.

The bite mark I've forgotten all about scarcely balances on the rim of the tub when Demi peels out of her nightie, then straddles my lap. I growl like a wild animal when the heat of her drenched pussy hits the crown of my cock. She's so desperate to be filled by me, she only drags my dick's head through the folds of her pussy two times before she lines up and drives home.

"Fuck, Demi. Fuck," I say with a moan. I'm incredibly turned on by her impatience, but I am also concerned as fuck that I might have hurt her. We don't always make love when we fool around, but I most certainly never aim to hurt her.

Any concerns that I've caused her pain fly out the window when she rises until the tip of my cock is braced at the entrance of her pussy before she slams back down. Her moans don't belong to a woman in pain. She's loving this as much as I am.

As her pussy sucks at my dick, sweat rolls down the gulley between her breasts. I feel her moan as much as I hear it when I lap up the salty blobs with my tongue before I shift my focus to her peaked nipples. I graze them with my teeth before sucking them into my mouth.

I fondle her breasts during her next five rises and falls before my body begs to get in on the action. My thighs scream in disgust when I raise my ass off the edge of the tub so I can meet Demi's grinds thrust for thrust. I did enough squats tonight to put Kim Kardashian's ass to shame, however, my quads come to the plate, preferring exhaustion over the possibility of ever disappointing Demi.

We pump, grind, and grunt on repeat until the pads of Demi's feet dig into my ass, and my grip on her nape is responsible for the speed of our fuck. We're in the middle of the bathroom where I kissed my crush for the first time, fucking the woman of my dreams. Things can't get better than this.

I take back what I said when Demi moans, "I'm close."

"Good," I reply before pumping into her faster, harder, and more controlled. "Because so the fuck am I."

Her moaned response to my reply almost sets me off. Cum races to the crest of my cock, but I hold back, refusing to come before Demi. She comes first, or I don't come at all. Those are the rules.

Not trusting of my legs to keep me upright when I give in to the sensation gripping my sack, I step us toward the wall opposite the tub that commenced my demise. Once Demi's back is braced against the sturdy backdrop, I drop my hand from her nape to her right hip, then arch my spine. The image of my cock pumping in and out of Demi's drenched slit keeps my orgasm at bay even when Demi succumbs to the tension crackling between us. Her juices are coating my cock, and her eyes are brimming with both lust and love. There's only one way this could get better.

Proof Demi is tapped into my inner-workings is exposed when the regaining of her senses is soon followed by her dismounting my cock and dropping to her knees. I bite out a curse word when she draws her lips over her teeth before she glides them over the crown of my cock. Her cheeks hollow partway down my veiny shaft before her tongue gets in on the action. She swivels it around the base of my dick before flattening it so she can take as much of me down her throat as she can.

I'm not ashamed to admit I blow my load the instant her lips get close to the cropped hairs spread across my pelvis. I've studied her sexual kinks in-depth so much the past two months, I know the difference between her wanting to give head and when she's craving the taste of my cum. The flare darting through her eyes today is the latter.

Thank fuck because if it was the former, Max's third maim of my ass tonight would have occurred long before the lusty gleam in Demi's eyes were satiated.

15

MADDOX

"Behave."

I give Max a stern finger point before leaning over to kiss Demi goodbye. Excluding the occasional ass gnawing, Max has settled into our dynamic well the past few days. He hates the male half of the population, but he thinks the sun shines out of Demi's ass, so I have no issues whatsoever with his overbearing protectiveness.

My ass—that's an entirely different story. It's still pissed about the five stitches and one big-ass needle it was handed after his last nip. Demi wanted to strangle the on-call doctor with his stethoscope when he suggested we put Max down. Fortunately for the doctor, Max kept a good four feet between Demi and him at all times so she never got the chance.

I thought Max hated me, but the pure disgust he had for the doctor made it obvious he tolerates me for Demi's sake. The doctor wasn't given the same courtesy. I'm still surprised he made it out of the cabin in one piece.

"Caidyn should be back around four. He got tied up at 'work.'" When I air quote my final words, Demi smiles. We're both suspicious he's been doing a lot more than rebuilding his business the past couple of weeks. "I could stay, but then I'll be late returning to take you to your shift at Petretti's."

I haven't left Demi alone for weeks. The thought alone has my stomach curdling, but I see it being worse if I could not chaperone her shift at Petretti's.

"I'll be fine," Demi assures me when my worries have me lingering in the living room like a bad smell. "Max won't let anything happen to me. Will you, Max?" I forget he has mental issues when he rests his fat head on Demi's thigh like he understands her. "Go do what needs to be done, then get back here. We've got a jam-packed weekend planned that leaves hardly any alone time. I need to squeeze in my fills whenever I can."

"Don't remind me," I grumble, my mood worsening.

We moved back into the cabin by the lake the day we adopted Max, but the front door is like a revolving door of family and friends. We have visitors at all times of the day and night, although there has been a notable absentee. Justine.

Patching things up with her is one of the tasks Demi and I plan to tackle this weekend. I've just got to get this run over with first.

"Please be careful," Demi implores while drifting her eyes over a smattering of bruises on my face. Last night's fight went a little longer than normal, and the impressive skills of my competitor are seen all over my face. Thank fuck, I still won. The prize money bumped up our escape funds by a cool twenty thousand. "I love you."

I flash Demi a cocky grin before replying, "I love you back." I get a two-second nibble on her lips before Max gives me my marching orders. His bark is so brutal and loud, it pierces my ears.

While wiggling a finger in my ear to lessen its ring, I say, "Keep our girl safe, Max."

He barks again—less aggressively this time around.

While shaking my head in disbelief about how smart he is, I pat his head. A head scratch won't show my appreciation of how fiercely he protects Demi, but since I'd most likely lose an arm if I got any closer, it is all I can give.

"Lock up behind me." With a nod, Demi stands to her feet to shadow my stalk to the door. Max follows suit, except he doesn't follow behind Demi. He walks in front of her, forever on the alert.

"Bye." I wave like a soft cock instead of kissing Demi like I really want to. "My damn dog is a cock blocker," I mumble to myself while galloping down the front stairs of the porch.

Once the deadbolt locks on the front door clang into place, I open the driver's side door of the Buick, then toss my gym bag inside.

Fifty minutes later, I arrive at the address cited on the tablet Rocco handed me this morning. I take a moment to ensure I have the right place before pulling the Buick down a long weaving driveway. The locations regularly change each run, but it's rare for the people behind the gates to alter. I guess Dimitri didn't take kindly to discovering his profits were being shaved by ten percent each shipment. Rocco's suspicions were right. The bricks I picked up at the start of the week were sneakily underweight.

"I'm here to pick up a delivery," I say to the skull-tattooed man by the main gate. He has a machine gun strapped to his chest and a cigarette dangling out of his mouth.

"Name."

Fuck, no. I'm not sharing personal information with him. I've got enough gangbangers on my plate. I don't need more.

"All the details are in here." I thrust the tablet his way. It's open on the screen that shows the shipment was ordered under the Petretti entity.

It seems as if I am a movie star with a highly recognized face when the business name on the top of the order sees the guard stumbling for the security gate panel. He pushes a button, granting me access to the fortress-like warehouse before announcing over the two-way speaker that the 'special order' has arrived.

The scene I drive toward replicates many I've witnessed the past couple of months. There are more guns than men, dark, dingy buildings, and a handful of skimpily dressed women loitering around like I may one day accept their many offers.

There's no fucking chance of that ever happening.

I'm not naïve. I know why they bombard me with sexual offers. They're hoping I won't see the men counting every dollar in my gym bag because they'd hate for me to let on to Dimitri that they don't trust him. Within a week, both the women paid to swarm me and the men bred to hate me, realized I don't trust Dimitri any more than them. So, for the most part, they stopped hounding me. I still get the occasional offer, but my perfected leave-me- the-fuck-alone face has kept them on the lower end of the scale.

"Stay in your vehicle," growls a tall man with thick biceps and a bald head.

I pop open my door, push past the throng of women circling me like sharks, then say, "I have orders to check the weight of the shipment before loading."

He doesn't look happy about my reply, but he either lets me check, or I leave without the goods. From how bulging my gym bag is, he can't afford for me to walk away.

"I just need to see the scales. That's it. Then I'll be gone."

I'd rather leave now, but beggars can't be choosers.

The man, I'd guess to be of Arabic descent, glares at me for two seconds before he jerks his head to the left. "Reload the bricks onto the scales." He returns his eyes to me. They're slit and full of anarchy. Let me assure you, the disdain is mutual. The women I generally deal with during runs weren't doped up like these ones are. They can barely walk, and I'm not going to mention the stained, dowdy nighties they're wearing. The last time I saw something so unfashionable was when my father went shopping for my mother. They were celebrating their thirty-second wedding anniversary, yet my mother still regifted my father's present to her mother-in-law.

"Don't touch anything."

I hold my empty hands out in front of myself before stuffing them into my pockets, assuring him my hands won't leave my sides.

Confident in my unvoiced pledge, he pivots on his heels and walks away. "This way."

I follow after him like the obedient, docile puppy I should have encouraged Demi to get. Then I could have trained him to hate every male on the planet *but* me. Alas, Demi fell in love with Max as quickly as she did me. That's got to mean something.

The further I shadow the man's walk, the more my brows pull together. A secondary building is behind the industrial-size warehouse. It appears to be more of a residence than a business premise. Thick-backed curtains shelter the first level of the property from prying eyes, but that isn't the only sign people live here, several shadows are projecting through the curtains— both tall and short.

I act as if I wasn't waving at a little girl I'd guess to be around seven or eight peering at me through a crack in a curtain when the goon showing me the way stops me in my tracks by splaying his hand across my chest. "Wait here."

I stray my eyes across the bland and desolate landscape. "Where am I meant to go?"

He doesn't answer my question. He just grunts before he heads in the direction of the residential building. His gigantic head is barely shadowed by an awning hanging over a steel door with numerous bolts when a lady with blonde hair and designer clothes steps over the threshold. I can't see her face, but I'm confident in saying she isn't here to welcome me with a cup of coffee and a freshly baked cake. She's so worked up, her neck muscles are pulled taut, making her appear scrawny and breakable.

My lips curl upward when her hands move a million miles an hour. If she isn't giving the man an ear-bashing, I'm not addicted to the taste of Demi's cum.

We both know that's far from the truth.

My curiosity piques when the unnamed man returns to my side. He's sweating like he personally sprinted from room to room to room to switch off the lights in the residence the blonde re-entered after scorning him. It's now shadowed in the darkness of this murky underworld.

Their endeavor to keep my focus away from the residence has me paying it more attention than the massive set of scales the head honcho recommences guiding me toward. The varying heights of the shadows seen before they switched off the lights make sense when my inconspicuous stalk has me stumbling onto hospital supplies of infant diapers, bottles, and formula stacked under a carport at the side of the building. There are more supplies than a standard family would need. Even someone with a dozen kids would have an issue using that number of diapers.

I snap my eyes to the right when the brute guiding our walk asks, "Satisfied?" He's standing in front of a set of brash scales that expose I'm moving more than my standard $100K of coke today.

Hoping to pull the wool over his eyes, I lower mine to the tablet Rocco supplies each run before twisting my lips. "Seems about right."

The man eyes me with suspicion for three heart-thrashing seconds before he clicks his fingers together two times. I return his stare when his minions jump to his unvoiced command. He has no resemblance to any Petretti I know, but the fact he orders his men around the same way catapults my suspicions to a record-breaking high.

"Do all the women around here dress like that?" I nudge my head to the women huddled at the side of the compound, unsure if they are coming or going.

The huge gent waits a beat before jerking up his chin. "It's how the boss likes them."

"Dirty?" I fire back before I can stop myself.

He gives me a look, one that says he doesn't appreciate my tone before he spits out, "Pure." He steps up to me, chest to chest. "None of those girls have been touched, so you should consider yourself lucky you were gifted one."

I hate admitting this, but his reference about the women being 'girls' is an accurate assumption of their age. I doubt a single one is of legal age.

It takes me working my next sentence through my head three times before my mouth finally relinquishes it. "Where would I take them if I wanted to… you know…" I can't say it. Pretending I want to cheat on Demi already has my skin crawling, so I can't see me expressing my lie without deceit highlighting my tone. My interrogation would be busted in an instant. "Is that what the residence is for? For the perks?"

Dark, oily brows pull together before the man shakes his head. "You'll have to take her in your car." He steps two paces away from me before asking, "Which one do you want? She won't let you have more than one."

"*She?* Your boss is a woman?" Now I know without a doubt that Col has nothing to do with this operation. He doesn't value the women who share his blood, so there's no way he'd let a woman head one of his operatives.

Before the man can answer me, he finds an excuse to end my interrogation. One of the men tossing bags of coke down the line misses his catch. Its fumble to the ground doesn't damage the goods, but the head goon acts as if he snorted the entire brick.

"You fuckin' idiot."

When he backhands the smaller, more subdued man, the mule stumbles backward. "Sorry, Maestro. I won't do it again."

His endeavor to get away from Maestro kicks up enough dust, a fleck of white pops up next to his feet. It could be nothing, but my intuition acts as if the paper-like material has next week's lotto numbers scribbled on it.

"It's fine." I huff while bending down to gather up the brick of coke, falsely portraying I'm annoyed my time is being wasted with dramatics. "It doesn't have a single dent." I thrust the brick into Maestro's face, effectively blocking my hand from his line of sight before tugging at the speckle of white piercing out of the ground. Since the canister its circling is deeply rooted in the recently laid gravel bed, its brisk removal leaves a divot in the previously flat landscape.

After standing to my feet, I adjust my stance so one of my shoes covers the hole my hunt left in the ground. "But to save face, bring my car around, and we'll load from here. We don't want any more incidents, do we?" When distrust flares through Maestro's eyes, I say, "Fine, I'll bring it around, then perhaps a handful of the women can occupy me during my two-second drive."

Maestro fans his hand across my chest, once again stopping me. Mercifully, his inability to share means I didn't get half a stride away from him. My cover isn't blown—yet.

"Wait here."

While nodding, I stuff my hands back into the pocket of my trousers like one side isn't filled with sand and a hard plastic matter shaped into a cylinder.

16

MADDOX

My eyes lift from a pill canister to Rocco when he asks, "Any issues? We've not used this manufacturer before, but pickings are slim when you cut your losses by severing more than fingers."

The nonchalant way he refers to murder would usually have me taking a nibble out of the bait he's dangling in front of me, but I'm off my game tonight. An empty prescription bottle shouldn't have my stomach twisted up in knots, but when you add it to the weirdness of tonight's exchange, a curdling stomach makes sense.

Furthermore, I swear I've seen this style of canister before—not just the shape and dimension, but the label printed on the front as well.

"Whatcha got there?" I try to shrug off Rocco's intuition, but he's a bigger snoop than me. He peers down at the canister for barely a second before his eyes rocket to mine. They looked pissed enough to kill with just a stare. "What are you doing with misoprostol?" He glares at me with nothing but pure hatred on his face. It matches the scowl Max gives me any time Demi shoos him out of our room so we can play sheet twister. "I thought Demi's miscarriage was an accident?"

"It was." I pause to work through my shock. When the delay gives me nothing but more unease, I mumble, "This isn't my prescription."

Rocco backhands me in the chest. His hit has more *oomph* than the playful ones he usually does. "Duh, fuckface. We're needed to make a baby, but we are positively *not* required to get rid of one." When confusion crosses his features, he nudges his head to the cracked canister in my hand. "That there is an abortion drug." A mask slips over his face before he asks matter-of-factly, "Where did you get it?"

"Nowhere important," I reply before I can stop myself, certain his interrogation will end a whole lot different than mine. "I was just curious as to how easy it is to get."

Rocco shrugs. "I'm more a cover-it-up-and-hope-for-the-best type of guy." He dumps my now empty gym bag into the passenger seat of the Buick before adding to the unease ridding the air of oxygen. "But if you know the right people, I don't see it being hard to get. Especially out there." He drops his eyes to the pharmacy name at the top of the label. "Shady shit *always* happens near Mercer Private."

"This script was issued by Mercer Private?"

He shakes his head. "But last check…" he doesn't mention his last check was because of Demi. "… that doctor is the on-call OBGYN at Mercer Private." He taps his index finger on a half legible name on the bottom of the prescription label. After waiting a beat, hopeful the delay will tap him into my inner-workings but leaving disappointed, Rocco says, "I'll get this unloaded so you can be on your merry way. Even with your brother *finally* showing up, I bet you're eager to get back to your girl. The first time you leave them alone is always the hardest."

Although I work my jaw from side to side, pissed about his snooping ways, my focus remains on the pill canister. The compound I visited tonight was in the opposite direction of Mercer Private, so why the fuck would someone travel over a hundred miles to have a prescription filled there? The canister is cracked and filled with sand, but the date on the label exposes it was only filled a little over two months ago, so I'm hedging bets it was for one of the many women—sorry, let me correct that—*girls* I saw tonight.

Too curious for my own good, I dig my cell phone out of my pocket before logging into the Safari app. The doctor's surname is a standard, everyday name, but when paired with Mercer Private, it pops up in a google search remarkably quick.

Dr. Franklin's credentials are listed as Rocco stated. He is the on-call OBGYN at Mercer Private, has a practice ten miles from the cabin Demi and I hid in for six weeks, and a yacht that looks way too fancy even if he were a world-renowned neurosurgeon.

After scrolling through hundreds of images of Dr. Franklin with a waif-thin blonde with big blue eyes, I add misoprostol into the search bar next to his name. I feel like I fall into a dark vortex when newspaper article after newspaper article pops up. They are all about a lawsuit Dr. Franklin faced after one of his patients died after taking an excessive amount of misoprostol.

She bled out on the lower level of her family home. She was only nineteen.

The horrid memories rolling through my head like a movie are too perverse for me to ignore. Before I consider the consequences of my actions, I ask Rocco, "If I supply Smith a name, could he get me an address?" When Rocco nods, I ask, "Now?"

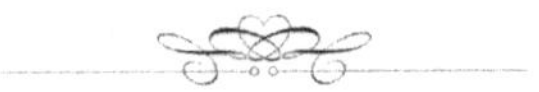

Twenty minutes later, I'm steering Rocco's Buick in the direction opposite of the Walsh lakeside cabin. Even if my love of the gas pedal shaves minutes off my time, I'll still cut it close to getting Demi to her shift on time. My curiosity hasn't skewed my priorities. Demi will *always* have the number one spot. I just have a feeling shelving my investigation will have a more detrimental effect to her well-being than missing a shift at Petretti's.

Besides, I have Demi's permission to look deeper into her miscarriage. Now is a prime time. Her uncle isn't breathing down my neck, Caidyn finally rocked up after an extra-long shift at 'work,' and the sting of the stitches in my ass reminds me there's no depth I won't push past to protect Demi.

By the time I arrive at Dr. Franklin's palatial home, the sun has set, and a baseball cap is covering a majority of my face. Dr. Franklin's elaborate residence doesn't fit in with the neighborhood. The suburbs surrounding Mercer Private are rundown and full of housing estates for the unemployed. His residence is three stories tall, boarded by a massive spiked fence, and there is more than one Doberman guarding acres of rolled turf.

I stop imagining how much damage four Dobermans could

do to my ass when something unexpectedly taps on the tinted window next to my head. After collecting my heart from the floor and resting my chin onto my chest, I roll down my window. The security officer who startled me doesn't have a visible gun, but I'm certain he's carrying. He has the arrogance of a man gunned up and ready to kill.

After stuffing his baton back into a steel loop around his belt, he asks, "Reason for your visit?"

I'm not known for thinking on the spot, however, it's a fight not to pat myself on the back when a brilliant idea smacks into me. "I'm here to collect a package for Nilon Enterprises." That was the name of the company on the purchase order I filled this afternoon.

The guard's brow quirks, advising he has heard the name before, but he plays it cool. "All collections are to be pre-arranged. Your name isn't down."

When he shoos me away with an arrogant wave of his hand, I get desperate. "Maestro organized it last minute with Dr. Franklin. It's for an urgent matter."

That gets his attention. "Maestro Sphitz?"

Certain I'm being tested, I reply, "If that's the name he's using this week, sure."

The guard laughs, assuming I'm being witty.

I'm not. I just know when I am being played.

After hitting a button to drop down the steel bollard in front of me, the guard says, "I'll ring ahead and let Dr. Franklin know you're on your way."

I swallow the brick his comment lodged into my throat before jerking up my chin. It gives him the opportunity to take in my lips and half my nose, but my eyes are still hidden.

Nerves take hold of my senses when I drive down the long gravel driveway. Mercifully, its length gives me time to settle the butterflies in my stomach, but it also means Dr. Franklin could reach Maestro to authenticate my ruse.

That will only end one way.

Badly.

A man matching the images I saw during my google search is standing on the front porch of his mega-mansion, grinning like a Cheshire cat. Confident I know the reason for his smile, I grab a bundle of the hundred-dollar bills Rocco hands me after every run before sliding out of my driver's seat. My theory that Dr. Franklin is all about greenback is proven without a doubt when his eyes locking in on the bundle of cash in my hand sees me gifted an invitation into his private abode.

His lack of personal security makes sense when the familiar burn of monitored cameras hone in on me when I enter his house. They follow our track across the foyer before they endeavor to zoom in on my face when I shadow Dr. Franklin into an office across from a massive media room.

This house isn't a mansion. It is a palace. The rooms are massive, the artwork is high-end however, it doesn't have a homey feel to it. It's cold and sterile, and I discover why that is when Dr. Franklin asks, "How far along is the patient?"

After swishing my tongue around my mouth to loosen up my words, I reply, "Only a couple of weeks."

Dr. Franklin grunts before murmuring, "Good. It will make this much more pleasant."

While he moves to a locked filing cabinet in the far corner of his office, I head for his desk. I rest my hip onto the edge of the massive carved wood design before folding my arms in front of my chest like I'm bored. His desk is spotlessly clean, but there are some telltale objects that announce most of his business practices are done from home. Patients' files are stacked next to a computer logged into Mercer Private's mainframe. It is next to a pair of stethoscopes and a machine that looks oddly similar to the portable ultrasound monitor Dr. Falgar used on Demi.

I stop inconspicuously seeking Demi's name on the patient medical records when Dr. Franklin asks a second sickening question. "How old is the patient?"

Known for pushing people outside of their comfort zones, I answer, "Nineteen."

I wait for him to flinch, glower, or take a moment to consider the fact he is the equivalent of scum on the bottom of the ocean. He does no such thing. He twists his lips, shrugs, then mutters, "Maestro does like them young. He just better hope Rimi doesn't find out. He doesn't let anyone touch the merchandise."

I choke on my spit. "Dimi?" I ask, certain I heard him wrong. That's the nickname those close to Dimitri use.

As his brows pull together, Dr. Franklin shakes his head. "No, I said Rimi." He steps closer to me, his stride as uneased as his facial expression when I lift my head enough he catches the color of my eyes. "What did you say your name was again?"

Busted!

"I didn't. *This* made it unnecessary to exchange salutations." I toss five one-thousand-dollar bundles onto his desk before fully raising my head. My back is facing the security camera, so even with my cover being blown by Dr. Franklin, I'm not worried about further prosecution. His equipment is as ancient as Agent Moses's. I highly doubt it has sound-capturing capabilities.

When Dr. Franklin lunges toward his desk—to secure a weapon, not my money—I pull out the gun I stuffed down my trousers partway here. Only a fool would enter a gun battle with their fists at the ready. "I wouldn't if I were you."

Dr. Franklin drops his half-filled prescription pad to the floor before stepping back with his hands held in the air. "None of the drugs are kept here—"

"I'm not here for narcotics."

He must see something on my face I didn't mean to express. "Who?"

I can't give common sense the chance to speak. I can hear the stomp of a man's boots in the distance. I have thirty seconds if I'm lucky. "Demi Petretti."

Dr. Franklin tries to act insolent. His endeavors are borderline.

"Have you heard of her before?"

He gives flattery a go. "Who hasn't? Everyone this side of the country knows of the Petrettis."

"Not *the* Petrettis." Sweat beads at his temples when I raise my gun from his stomach to his chest. "Demi. *Specifically.*"

When he shakes his head, I aim my gun at the crinkle between his brows. "One accidental twitch, and you'll be dead."

It dawns on me things occur a lot sooner when you use violence instead of reason. I've barely curled my finger around the trigger when Dr. Franklin blubbers like a narc, "She came to me desperate for an untraceable prescription of misoprostol."

"Bullshit!" I yell, my voice a roar.

"It's true," he replies just as loudly. "She couldn't have her uncle finding out she was pregnant. If she had gone through his men for a solution to her predicament, he would have found out."

"You're lying. She was with me the entire time." *She also wanted our baby as much as me,* but since I can't say that out loud, I keep it locked up inside of me like a vault.

Dr. Franklin shakes his head. "She came to me. She sat right there." He points to the chair across from his desk, hoping it will distract me from the lies I see in his eyes. "I have the details she gave me."

With my head murky with confusion, I allow him to move toward the stack of patient files on his desk. It is stupid for me to do. He wasn't moving for a weapon earlier. He wanted the distress button under his desk—the exact button that sounds an alarm a good three seconds before my boot forces him away from it.

As the stomps charging my way double in loudness, Dr. Franklin sails across the room. He lands on top of an open filing cabinet drawer with a groan. With how hot my blood is with annoyance, I'm tempted to act as if I am as immoral as Col and Dimitri. I wouldn't hesitate if I didn't have a million questions still to ask. I've also run out of time. A security officer with thick biceps and an angry scowl is blocking the doorway of Dr. Franklin's office, leaving me no choice but to exit via the open window on my left.

My lungs heave from exhaustion when I run across the dewy ground to the Buick. I slip into the driver's seat and crank the ignition in under ten seconds. Gravel kicks up beneath the Buick's tires before they rocket down the driveway. Their brutal crunch along with the pounding of my pulse should drown out everything else, so you can imagine my shock when I hear Dr. Franklin shout for the guards to let me go.

Who does that?

Who in their right mind lets a maniac who pulled a gun on them go free?

With my confusion at a pinnacle, I take a windy corner two miles from Dr. Franklin's residence too sharply. The tires slide out the Buick's back end when I hit the loose gravel at a speed too fast to be safe. I correct my error quickly, but the closeness of the Buick's grill to a massive tree trunk has me pulling off the road for a breather. Getting in a wreck won't help anyone.

The darkness of a cloud-filled night means it takes me a few moments to recognize where I am. I'm half a mile from the cabin Demi and I camped at for six weeks—if that.

A shiver rolls up my spine when I consider how close I had Demi to a monster. I thought I was getting her away from one. I had no clue she was only miles away from evil. A different type of evil than her uncle, but still evil, nonetheless.

Still needing answers, I guide the Buick toward the loaned cabin instead of the family cabin where Demi is waiting for me. The eerie silence surrounding the cabin when I drive down the driveway swirls the lunch Demi prepared for us before my run.

After pulling up next to the front porch, I tug my coat in close, then climb the entry stairs. I haven't been here since I thought I had lost the love of my life, and my breakthrough of the threshold this time around doesn't come without contro-versy. The faintest scent Demi's hair got from our many romps here is lingering in the air, but a much more unpleasant smell is overriding it.

I never realized how strong the scent of blood is until I

stumbled onto Demi in the shower. It's a scent that will never leave me. Despite wishing otherwise, it will plague my nightmares for years to come. Even more so when my push on the bathroom door of the master suite has the exact smell I'm terrified of confronting me head-on.

Caidyn said his 'friend' rarely uses this cabin, and his assumption is proven accurate when I drag my eyes over the shattered shower stall glass still scattered across the tiled floor. Even the marks my bloody fists left on the tiles remain. It is as if time stood still. Nothing has changed.

After taking a moment to remember things are starkly different from what they once were—Demi is both alive and safe—I search the expansive marble counters near the vanity sink. When I fail to find the canister of vitamins I saw behind the positive pregnancy tests when I endeavored to get Demi responsive and alert, I search the drawers in the vanity before rummaging through a half-full bin on my left, mindful the canister could have fallen during my panic.

"Fuck it!" I mutter under my breath when the tip of my finger is sliced by a shard of glass hiding in the bottom of the bin.

My eyes jackknife to the right when a soft, full-of-angst voice says, "Serves you right." Demi is standing in the doorway of the bathroom. Her arms are folded in front of her chest, and Max is standing at her left. "I told him there was no way you'd be out here, that if you had questions you wanted to ask me, you'd come directly to me." She huffs instead of crying. It doesn't appear to be an easy feat. "What a fool I was."

"I'm not here investigating you—"

"Then what are you doing, Maddox? You were meant to do your run, then come home."

Her shouted words stir Max, but his response is nothing compared to the angst my reply hits her with, "I'm trying to work out what happened to our baby. What *really* happened."

The crackling of her voice exposes she is on the verge of crying, but she maintains her composure—just. "We had a miscarriage, Maddox. It occurs all the time."

"It does, but how often does it occur an hour after taking a tablet you knew nothing about?" I dig the canister I found at the warehouse out of my pocket before showing it to Demi. "The canister your vitamins were in looked like this—"

"*All* pill canisters look like that."

I continue speaking as if she never interrupted me. "The prescription label on this canister was issued by a doctor who is being investigated for malpractice." I wait for her to absorb the half legible doctor's name on the label of the canister before adding, "He doesn't prescribe vitamin tablets, Demi. He hands out abortion pills like candy during Halloween."

Demi's lips quiver when she whispers, "He was right. You think I purposely hurt our baby."

Her accusation hits me like a ton of bricks, but it won't stop me from saying, "No. That isn't close to what I think." My heart falls from my chest when she ends my attempt to step closer to her by slicing her hand through the air. This is the first time she's ever denied me. I don't fucking like it—not one little bit. "You also shouldn't be *listening* to anything Rocco says. You said he was the one who gave you the tablets, so he could be endeavoring to cover his tracks by placing a massive barrier between us."

"He did bring me the vitamins," she fires back, both angered she needs to defend herself and devastated. "But Rocco wouldn't do that, Maddox. He'd *never* hurt me like that."

"Not even if he was ordered to by Dimitri?" Her shock freezes her long enough I can bridge the gap between us. Max keeps me a good two feet back, but I'm close enough for Demi to see the gut-wrenching truth in my eyes when I say, "Someone *purposely* set out to hurt our baby. If it wasn't you, a member of your family is the next logical suspect." I realize how badly I fucked up when a heartbreaking flare darts through Demi's eyes. "I didn't mean it was you. I talk out my ass when I'm tired. You know that."

"Yeah, I do know that," Demi replies, making me hopeful I haven't shoved my foot into my mouth too badly this time around. "But I also know that is when you're the most honest." She ignores the rapid shake of my head. "How about I make things easy for you, Maddox?" Her next set of words break her heart as much as they do mine. "It is *my* fault our baby is dead. *I am to blame.*" She jabs her fingers into her chest. "Because you were right. *I* did take the tablet stupidly believing it would help our baby. *I* also slipped and bumped my head, so perhaps *I* am responsible for the death of our child."

"Demi—"

She cuts my reply short by spinning away from me and walking outside.

I'm on her heels in under a second. "Where are you going?"

"To do my shift at Petretti's. Late is better than never, right?"

I wait until she has Max clipped into the passenger seat of Caidyn's jeep before grabbing her arm. I only need to run my fingertip down her nose once to calm her down. Once she's calm, she'll realize I'm not the opposition. We belong on the same team.

My hand doesn't get within an inch of Demi's nose before she shouts, "Don't!" Her one word cracks out of her mouth like a whip. "I drove here to prove to myself Dimitri is a lying piece of shit." I don't know what shocks me more, confirmation she's been communicating with her cousin or the words she says next. It may be a combination of both. "I'm leaving having no clue who the hero of this story is."

Stealing my chance to reply, she jogs around to the driver's side door, slips behind the steering wheel, then drives away.

17

—————

DEMI

As I turn onto the street where Petretti's Restaurant is located, I drag my hand across my wet cheeks. I'm sure I look like an absolute wreck. I've been sobbing for almost two hours straight. When Dimitri called me out of the blue to update me on a conversation Maddox and Rocco had in his presence, in my head, I called him every name under the sun. Nothing he said made any sense. Although Maddox had raised suspicions about our miscarriage previously, not once were his distrusts directed at me, so I was more than confident Dimitri was trying to cause trouble.

I should have left it at that, but over the past two months, Maddox's annoying traits have started to rub off on me. I told myself a dozen times not to log into the Find My Phone app he installed on his MacBook Air, that it was only to be used in emergency situations, but as Maddox likes the say, 'curiosity killed the cat, but satisfaction brings it back.'

It didn't even take a second for me to realize which direction Maddox was traveling when his cell phone popped up on the map. The blue dot was surrounded by bushland I memorized like the back of my hand while staring out the window, awaiting Maddox's return every Friday night.

I want to pretend I grabbed my coat and borrowed Caidyn's jeep because I was keen for a game of naked Twister, but that would be a lie. Dimitri's words wouldn't stop playing on repeat in my head.

"He wants to place the burden on anyone's shoulders but his."

"When a man is grieving, no one is safe. I never thought he'd suspect you, though."

"Will you stay with him when he looks at you differently?"

"Every time he looks at you, he'll remember what he lost."

That last one killed me the most. Not just because I already see the hurt in Maddox's eyes, but because it's there for more than the loss of our baby. He killed for me. He ended another's man life. The way he looks at me has already changed because our relationship forced him to become someone he never wanted to be.

I push my despair to the back of my mind when I pull Caidyn's jeep into the lot behind Petretti's. Since I'm three hours late for my shift, I park in the only spot remaining before clipping Max's lead onto his collar. "Please behave tonight, Max. I don't need more trouble."

He barks as if he understands me before he climbs out of Caidyn's jeep on my heel.

We make it halfway across the dusty lot before an accented voice from behind bristles the hairs on both Max's nape and mine. "I should have freed you a long time ago. Butterflies are always more enticing once they've been released from the cocoon."

My uncle hisses at Max as if he is a cat before he paces closer to me. His skin is very white for a man who just spent the last two months soaking up the sun in a coastal community in Italy.

The closer my uncle gets to me, the more vicious Max's bark becomes. My uncle tries to act unaffected by Max's foamy growl. It is all an act. The fact he stays a good three to four feet back exposes this, much less his shouted warning, "Shut him up before I shut him up permanently!"

His roar works Max up more. He growls and barks and yanks on his lead so much, it takes everything I have to hold him back, and even then, he gets close enough for my uncle's goon to punish his disobedience with his boot. He kicks Max in the stomach, breaking my heart and Max's psychosis at the same time. He whimpers in pain before he shuffles back to stand at my side, but not once does he remove his eyes from my uncle.

With my heart still in tatters from my argument with Maddox, I speak before considering the consequences of my actions. "He's a puppy! A baby! You didn't have to kick him!"

My uncle looks torn between laughing and slapping me across the face. He loses the chance to do either of those things when a second familiar voice sounds through the quiet of the night. This one is more Americanized than my uncle's but just as chilling.

Shit! I inwardly scream when four sets of eyes shift in the direction Dimitri's voice came from. He isn't alone. The passenger he's helping into his car idling at the side entrance of

Petretti's has distinguishable red locks, a traffic-stopping face, and an aura that commands attention.

All the Walsh siblings have soul-stealing characteristics—even the female share.

I return my jaw to its original position when my uncle gabbers out, "That's an interesting development, isn't it."

Don't misconstrue. He isn't asking a question. He'd never value my opinion enough to care what I thought.

I feel Max's growl more than I hear it when my uncle leans in close enough I smell garlic in his breath. "I bet you didn't consider adding her name onto the list when you *went against me!*" He screams his last three words into my face. "After everything I did for you, you turned my own son against me!"

I shake my head in blatant denial. "Everything Dimitri did, he did of his own accord. I had no say about any of it." If I did, you can be assured Maddox wouldn't be running drugs for him. Sloane's safety is my debt to pay, so if I had it my way, only I would be paying it off.

I wordlessly pray for my uncle to take his anger out on me when he murmurs, "You should be more cautious with your stipulations when you make a deal with the devil."

Dust kicks up around my feet when I follow his race across the shadowed lot. "Justine isn't a part of this. None of her family is." Desperate to stop him before he irreparably scars another member of the Walsh tribe, I drop Max's leash to the ground, then grab hold of my uncle's hand. "Hit me, mark me, torture me, but please don't hurt Justine. She doesn't deserve your anger. I do! Hit me!"

The back of my uncle's hand only just brushes my cheek when Max launches into action. He clamps his jaw down on his wrist, viciously mauling him as Maddox has dreamed of doing for months.

Just as the tangy smell of copper filters into the air, the ricochet of a gun being fired echoes through the somewhat isolated space. The bang dislodges Max from my uncle's arm, but it does little to subdue his protective stance. He darts his eyes between my uncle and his head goon, Mario, unsure which is the lesser of two evils—the man carrying a gun or the one glaring at me like he'd sell his soul for the chance to torture me.

"You should have picked your battles more wisely." My stomach gurgles when my uncle spits out, *"Famiglia prima di tutto."*

Family first of all was our ancestors' motto. My grandfather lived by it, and my father honored it, but my uncle has done nothing but taint it. He never puts his family first. It's an impossible task for a man as selfish as him.

After a final snarl, my uncle clicks his fingers together two times before sliding into the back seat of his Audi town car. I'm so shaken with feared adrenaline, it takes my uncle's vehicle leaving the lot before I can dig my cell phone out of my pocket to dial a familiar number.

The spike of my pulse is heard in my shallow breaths when Maddox answers my call not even a ring later. "I'm two minutes away, five tops. I had to veer by the cabin to pick up Caidyn. He's pissed you stole his jeep again. Not as much as he is worried, but pissed, nonetheless."

"You're coming here?" I ask through a sob.

Maddox breathes out heavily like he's disappointed I'd even contemplate that he wouldn't follow me to the end of the earth.

"Yes, of course. I swear, Demi, I'd never accuse you of hurting our baby. I just want answers, that's all."

I appreciate what he's saying, and I'm certain once I have a moment to catch my breath, I'll understand it even more, but right now, things we can't change shouldn't be in the forefront of our minds. Justine's safety should be.

"My uncle is here in Hopeton. I just saw him." I didn't realize you could hear blood pressure rising until now. Maddox's pulse sounds as if it is going through the roof.

His foot does the opposite. As the Buick's engine roars to life, so does the panic in his voice. "Did he see you?"

"Yes, but you don't need to worry about me. Max protected me." On instinct, my hand darts down to pat Max's head. "He's going after Justine."

"What?" Maddox and Caidyn gabble out at the same time, announcing I'm on speakerphone.

"She just left Petretti's with Dimitri. Col saw them. He told me I should have picked my battles better." I suck in the quickest breath to ensure I don't faint from a lack of oxygen before pushing on, "I think he's going to hurt Justine in retaliation for not being able to hurt us. He mentioned our agreement with Dimitri."

With Maddox's silence weighing heavy on both Caidyn's and my chest, Caidyn asks, "Do you know where Dimitri is taking Justine?"

Even though they can't see me, I shake my head. "He's in his Hennessey, though. It's the only one of its kind this side of the country."

I hear Caidyn swallow before he asks, "Which direction did they go?"

I take a moment to gather my bearings. This is the first time in my life I'm grateful I was raised in Hopeton. I know where I am and which direction Dimitri took off to. "Northwest."

"He's taking her home." Maddox waits for the gurgle of Caidyn's stomach to halve in volume before finalizing, "To *his* home."

I've often wondered if siblings can communicate without words. The silence sounding down the line assures me they can. Even without a word being uttered, their wordless conversation is unequivocally reassuring.

After a couple of seconds of deliberation, Maddox says my name in a husky tone, "Demi…"

He only mutters my name, but it's the words he doesn't speak I hear the loudest. "It's okay. I'm safe. Go! Make sure Justine is as well."

A faint woosh sounds down the line like he's hesitantly nodding. "Stay at Petretti's." The hesitance in his tone reveals he loathes the idea of me being at Petretti's without him, but he is also aware I am safe here because this is as much my stomping ground as it is Col's. "I'll come get you as soon as I can."

"Okay." I lick my lips, hating the angst in his tone but happy I know a way to eradicate it instantly. "I love you, Maddox."

His sigh this time around is in relief instead of regret. "I love you back, baby. Don't ever forget that, all right?"

"I won't. I'll never forget," I choke out through a clog of tears.

It takes four heartbreaking seconds for Maddox to end our call, but only two seconds for me to crumble to the ground with a howl.

18

MADDOX

"*There!*"

Caidyn's head whacks into the Buick's tinted window when I yank on the steering wheel in the direction he's pointing. We dangerously careen past a stream of vehicles sitting between us and a prototype Hennessey Venom F5.

"Plant your foot to the floor," Caidyn demands when Dimitri's brutal speed sees him getting several car lengths in front of us.

"I fuckin' am. This is as fast as this thing goes."

I throw the gearstick into third before backing up my demand for the Buick to go faster by pumping the gas pedal three times. The engine almost chokes on the sudden influx of gasoline, but like all things, when in fear for their life, it performs miracles. We rocket toward Dimitri like we injected nitrous oxide into the fuel lines.

I mimic Dimitri's butt-clenching maneuvers until we slot in behind him three miles out from Sandy Plains. When our eyes lock and hold in the rearview mirror of his sports car, my jaw grits. He's got his game face on—the very face he wears anytime Fien's name is whispered in his ear. He isn't backing down for anything or anyone.

After working through the gears, I pull the Buick into the emergency lane. Dimitri's stern expression exposes there's no chance of him seeing sense through the madness, but I'm hopeful as fuck Justine isn't wearing her stubborn pants today.

"Fuck!" I push out with a roar when Dimitri suddenly brakes before he whizzes onto an off-ramp.

I slam on my brakes just as quickly, but the Buick doesn't have the grunt needed to reach the set of lights Dimitri's ride just sailed through before the light switches to amber.

"You won't make it," Caidyn cautions when I increase my pressure on the gas pedal instead of weakening it.

"I will. There's a gap between the bus and the truck."

While checking his seat belt is properly latched, Caidyn shakes his head. "That's a scooter gap, not a fucking Buick's."

"I'll make it. I swear. I don't have time to brake." The longer Demi is at Petretti's, the more her safety is compromised. That alone sees me flattening my foot to the floor. I'm not just racing to save my baby sister from a monster, my girl's safety is on the line as well.

As we zoom over the white line I should be yielding at, Caidyn murmurs, "Fucking hell. I'm about to die."

His rapid blinks match the frantic flash of the truck driver's headlights when he warns me that he can't slow down. We'll either dart between him and a minivan with not even an inch to spare or plow headfirst into the side of a semi. I really fucking hope I haven't miscalculated our run.

"Clench your ass cheeks, Caidyn. I'm about to teach you how to fly."

When we sail across the intersection a hair's breadth in front of the grill of a semi, the truck driver's horn shrills through my ears as loudly as Caidyn's panicked roar. "Jesus-fucking- Christ!"

The Buick's underbody crunches into the asphalt on the other side a mere second before the scent of burning rubber lingers in the air. We're alive, being abused by motorists, and I'm reasonably sure I just shit myself.

When I chuckle about my last reference, Caidyn looks at me as if I'm insane. "I don't give a fuck what Mom says, I'm scheduling you an appointment with Dr. Avery the instant this is over." My laughter is ill-timed, but there's no holding it back when he whispers to himself, "I think I just shit myself."

While he checks his pants for wetness, I scan the street seeking any sign as to which way Dimitri went. This area is miles away from his mega-mansion on Sandy Plains road, both in distance and stature. It's rundown and riddled with homeless people.

Well, so I thought.

"Is that a Windham M-Lok?" Caidyn asks after taking in the same confronting visual as me. "They're eighteen hundred dollars a pop. How the fuck can a homeless man afford that?"

I've never been more grateful for my inability not to be a hothead when the man Caidyn is gawking at spots our stalk. He pushes back the cardboard concealing the second half of his expensive gun before recognition dawns on his face as to why our ride is so familiar. Rocco's ride instantly changes the expression on his face. If we were in

Caidyn's jeep, we would have been sprayed with bullets by now.

Once Caidyn reaches the same conclusion as me, he mutters, "We're heading in the right direction."

I jerk up my chin in agreement before seeking more hidden militiamen in the tented community. They guide our route through the backstreets of Hopeton. It's a painstakingly slow process, but the dividends are undeniable when it leads us to a large concrete structure in the far west corner of the suburb. The men in front of this compound don't hide their weapons. They're in plain view for all to see while they walk the fence line surrounding both the warehouse setting and Dimitri's pricy ride.

"What now…" Caidyn's words shift to silence when the shrill of my cell phone rumbles out of the Buick's speakers. "Is that him?"

I shouldn't know who he's referencing since he only spoke three short words, however, I do. His voice had way too much disdain for me to believe he was referring to anyone but Dimitri.

Confident Dimitri is calling to gloat about his victory, I push the call button before growling out, "I swear to fuckin' God, Dimitri, if you don't bring my sister out here immediately, I'm going to wring your fucking neck—"

He cuts off my tirade with words much more threatening. "If you want your sister to get out of tonight alive, I suggest you shut your mouth and listen to me." The pure honesty in his tone stills both Caidyn's and my chests. "Tell the goon manning the gate that you need to go to the Gauntlet, give him the passcode 'cannon.' When you arrive, fall to your knees and fucking beg. Say anything and everything Col wants to hear."

"Dimitri…"

When shock steals my words, Caidyn takes up the slack. "What the fuck is going on?"

My heart launches into my throat when Dimitri replies as if Caidyn's question was asked by me. "You said you'd die for your sister, right?"

Caidyn's brows pull together when I answer, "Yeah."

The clutter of an old steel door being slammed shut sounds down the line before Dimitri says, "Tonight is your chance to prove that. Your life for hers, Maddox. I don't see Col taking any less."

I stare at the Buick's dashboard for the next several seconds, unmoving and unspeaking, then all of a sudden, a light inside my head switches on.

"Stay here," I say to Caidyn when he follows my scramble out of the Buick.

"Like hell, Maddox. That's *our* sister in there."

I push him back three places when he attempts to beat me to the gate. "That's right. That is *our* sister in there, but she's there because of *me*, so it's *my* responsibility to get her out."

He shoves me back just as firmly. "I rank higher than you."

"How so?"

With flaring nostrils and balled hands, he gets up in my face. "I'm older, which means I rank higher."

"This has nothing to do with rank, Caidyn! You heard what Dimitri said, it's my life or Justine's. Me or her. Pick."

He looks like he wants to be sick, his repulsion perverse

enough for him to stumble back two paces. "I'm not fucking picking. I could never..." A shudder finalizes his reply.

"Then you understand why you need to stay here. I have no trouble picking." I strive to keep my expression neutral when saying, "But I need to know someone will be there for Demi, Caidyn. I need to know she'll be taken care of as she deserves." I choke on my next set of words. "If it can't be me, I want it to be you." I don't mean sexually. I mean in the essence of a brother-in-law protecting his sister-in-law. Caidyn cares for Demi, but there isn't an ounce of sexual ambiguity behind his mutual admiration. "Women always come first, Caidyn. It's what our father taught us."

"No, Maddox." He shakes his head so fast I'm sure I can hear the rattling of his brain against his skull. "This isn't what he meant."

When I step up to him chest to chest, eyes to eyes, brother to brother, relief engulfs me. Although he is verbally denying my request, his eyes say the opposite. He'll have my back no matter what because that is what the Walsh brothers do. It is how our father raised us.

"It has to be me, Caidyn. I need to take responsibility for my actions."

He hates that I'm right, but he won't announce it out loud. His job as my big brother means he's meant to protect me as I'm endeavoring to protect Justine, but that's null and void when the fuck-up lands solely on my shoulders.

Caidyn takes a moment to stray his eyes to the concrete bunker on his right before he eventually jerks up his chin. The quiet shrouding the compound aided in his agreement. It doesn't give me the same level of comfort. Nothing good ever comes from long bouts of silence. "But we'll have words about this once you're out. I want it noted that I'm not fucking happy, Maddox. Not with you and not with Justine. I warned her about this."

I get where his frustration stems from, but I don't have time to assure him his points are valid. "Wait here. I'll be right out with Justine." The ease of my statement would have you convinced I'm walking into a locker room full of pimple-faced teens instead of a compound filled with militiamen willing to do anything their commander orders. "Then we'll take it from there. We *will* get through this." I squeeze his shoulder in silent support. I wish I could offer him more comfort than that, but time isn't in our favor, and men like Caidyn need more than a bro-hug to see them through a crisis. "It's what we do." I squeeze his shoulder for the second time before tapping my knuckles over his heart. "We'd rather destroy ourselves than let our siblings experience our pain."

Stealing his chance to reply, I give him the quickest bro-hug, then sprint for the guarded steel gate.

"Stop right there." My chest lights up with more than the scope of a single assault rifle. "This is private property."

With my hands held out in front of me in a non-defensive manner, I say, "I'm here for the Gauntlet." I have no clue if the Gauntlet is a place or a thing. Men in this industry like naming themselves after objects, so it is highly possible it could be a person. "The password is cannon."

The armed guard drifts his eyes in the direction I came from before returning them to my face. "Are you carrying any weapons?"

When I shake my head, grateful as fuck I shoved my gun

into the glove compartment of the Buick when Caidyn raced down the stairs of our family cabin, the guard requests for me to raise my shirt.

Once he has visually cleared me of weapons, he lifts his chin, signaling for a second man in a security box next to the gate to open it. The spiked barrier Dimitri's vehicle is parked behind jerks open only just enough for me to squeeze through.

I'm subjected to a quick frisk search by goon number two before the head goon signals for a third armed man to join our trio. "He's going to the Gauntlet. Take him straight there."

The excited flare darting through the man's eyes has me wondering if the Gauntlet is a woman. If it isn't, what excuse does he have for the thirsty glint forming in his eyes?

"This way." He nudges his head to the door at the side of the concrete structure before heading in the direction he nudged.

After flashing a final glance Caidyn's way, I fall into step behind the goon. My heart is raging, and I'm sweating profusely. Nothing good ever comes from eerie silence, and that's all we're being bombarded with right now. Excluding the five men manning the entrance, there doesn't appear to be another soul nearby.

The reason for the quiet smacks into me when we step down a set of concrete stairs. At least two hundred men are in a bunker-like room at the bottom of a spiral staircase. There are also a handful of women, none of which have lava-red hair. They're all peering at a dome in the middle of the deathly black space, laughing and cheering at whatever spectacle is occurring in the glass shoebox-shaped arena.

As they surge toward the thick windowpanes, the roars of the crowd remind me of scenes from the *Gladiator* movie.

They're thirsty for blood like hungry vultures circling a carcass. Inhuman, immorally corrupt fuckers I sentence to burn in hell when I realize who their attention is rapt on.

The Gauntlet isn't a person. It's a torture chamber. A horror skit more unimaginable than you could ever comprehend, and my baby sister is in the middle of it.

"J!"

My stomach launches into my throat when my shout of Justine's nickname is overtaken by the vicious growl of a dog trained to attack. When his leash is unclipped from his studded collar, he charges across the room like his hunger for carnage is as cruel as the crowds. He isn't like Max. He wasn't trained to protect women. He was trained to kill. The viciousness of his charge is indicative enough, much less the way his teeth rip through Justine's dress like a hot knife through butter.

I push through the throng of people separating us, uncaring of who I shove to get by. I've always said I'm not a killer, that I'm just a man who wants to do some good for his community. That's null and void right now. The pure hatred shredding through my veins could take down an army. Not even a bullet could slow me down.

"No!" I bang my fist against the glass when the Rottweiler's teeth sinking into the back of Justine's leg causes her knees to buckle out from underneath her. She lands on the blood-splattered floor with a pained gurgle. Her face is wet with tears, and her dress is already soaked through with blood.

The smallest snippet of relief hits me when Justine's survival instincts kick in. She kicks out her leg, dislodging the dog from her ribs before rolling into a ball so she can protect her face and skull with her arms.

As the terrified screams of my baby sister shred my eardrums, I circle the dome, seeking an entrance. She got in there somehow, but from this viewpoint, there's no visible entry point.

Seconds feel like minutes when I scan the crowd, desperate enough to follow through with Dimitri's suggestion. My sister is being torn apart by a vicious animal. Begging is very much on the agenda.

Some of the crowds' focus shifts from watching Justine's attack to me when I spot Col on a podium at the back of the space. He has a prime view of the proceedings, and his smug grin tethers the last bit of my soul. A woman is being murdered with a viciousness eviler than Satan himself, yet he's smiling like he's at an award show, being honored with the highest gong.

If I could get Justine out of this alive *and* slit Col's throat, I'd give it everything I have. Regrettably, the blood in your veins doesn't need to be drained for you to die. The cries of your baby sister on the brink of death are enough to stop any man's heart.

It takes me breaking one of Col's goon's noses and another's ribs to get close enough to Col to fall to my knees, but when I do, the self-righteous grin he was wearing catapults to full-blown arrogance. He's craved this moment for years. I guarantee it.

"Please," I beg from his feet with wet eyes and a gun butted against my head. "She isn't a part of this. She should have *never* been a part of this." My comment is for both Demi and Justine. "I'll do anything you want. Name your price."

Col looks down his nose at me. "It's too late for that."

"No, it's not. I'm still useful to you. I can help you." I thrust my hand in the direction Justine's cries are whimpering from. "This will benefit no one. What will her death possibly achieve?"

It dawns on me that Demi is right, Justine is enduring our punishment when Col shouts, "Fear, respect, and integrity! All the things I lost when you failed to keep your mouth shut!"

He glances over my shoulder, smiling when the image of a bloody and almost unconscious Justine reflecting in his massively dilated pupils causes me to gag. She has protected her face and neck well from the Rottweiler, but she's in too much pain to remain lucid. Her willpower is wilting. She's minutes from death.

I'm not the only one noticing this.

Col is just as aware.

"The light in her eyes is almost all gone."

Desperate, I beg more. "I'll give you anything. My life for Justine's. My soul. My entire fucking existence. I'll give you anything you want."

"Her?" He doesn't need to mention Demi's name for me to know who he's referencing. I can see it in the psychopathic blackness in his eyes. He wanted me on my knees, but his desires have nothing to do with my sister and everything to do with the woman I love.

When Col spots my headshake, the growls of a dog in the midst of a horrifying attack ramp up. Like the scene could possibly get any more violent, the Rottweiler tosses Justine around the blood-soaked space like she's a rag doll. The flop of her limbs as she endures bite after bite after bite severs my last nerve. I'm dead—wholly and without limitation.

"Okay."

Col holds a single finger in the air, momentarily stopping the proceeding before lowering his eyes to mine. "What did you say?"

I swallow the massive lump in my throat before muttering in a dull, unrecognizable tone, "I said okay. I'll give you anything you want. *Anything* at all."

"Very well." With the grin of a man who was just granted his greatest wish, Col clicks his fingers together two times. A second later, wood panels on his right pop open, exposing a small hidden stairwell that leads to the entrance of the glass dome Justine is being mauled in.

"Do be careful," Col mutters with a smirk when I stand to my feet and race toward the hidden entrance. "Menace is known to bite when he feels threatened."

19

DEMI

Max's head pops up at the same time as mine when the shrill of my cell phone echoes in the eerie quietness. I've been hiding out in the office at Petretti's for the past six hours, panicked out of my mind. Delayed satisfaction isn't something Maddox ever participates in. He is as impatient as he is sexy. He'd never leave me in the dark as long as he has unless it was imperative, so I'm not just on the verge of a breakdown, I am seriously considering doing something stupid. I'm contemplating reaching out to my uncle. He isn't a man I should seek help from in a crisis but considering almost all the knot in my stomach centers around him, I don't have much choice but to act recklessly.

He's able to restart my heart just as easily as he can destroy it.

I suck in my first full breath in hours when the screen of my phone flashes up a familiar face. "It's him. It is Maddox," I say to Max like he can understand me.

Through shuddering hands and an extremely heavy heart, I slide my finger across the screen of my phone before squashing it to my ear. "You scared the shit out of me. Is Justine okay? Are you okay? Did you see my uncle—"

A familiar voice interrupts my interrogation.

Sadly, it isn't the one I'm desperate to hear.

"It's Caidyn."

I pull my phone down to check the image on the screen. It is as seen only moments ago—the sneaky picture I snapped of Maddox one afternoon when he was deep in thought. His beard is thicker than it usually is, and his reddish-blond brows are pinched together as he peers out the window of the cabin, but it is very much the man I recall anytime memories of the past two months lift my lips into a smile.

After returning my phone to my ear, I ask, "Why do you have Maddox's phone?" I try to keep the angst out of my tone. I miserably fail.

"A surgeon found it in Justine's tattered clothes." The siren of an ambulance bounding out of the speakers of my cell phone gobbles up my petrified sigh. "I don't have time to go into details right now, Demi. I just need you to listen to me very carefully." Caidyn can't see me, but he must hear my nod because he resumes speaking without waiting for verbal confirmation. "After the surgeon updated us on Justine's condition, I searched Maddox's phone for clues on what had happened. I found a note in the message section of his phone. It was dated an hour before Justine was carried out to me." My head is swirling. Surgeons. Conditions. Justine being carried out. What the fuck did my uncle do? "The message was addressed to you, Demi."

"What did it say?" I'm surprised I can talk with how hard my heart is raging, and the situation worsens when Caidyn mutters, "It's just one of those days, Demi. I'll love you back for eternity. Don't ever forget that."

"It was written exactly like that? 'It's just one of those days?'"

"Yes," Caidyn answers before adding, "When we were kids, that was Maddox's SOS when he needed help."

"I remember." Tears careen down my cheeks when I recall Maddox including me in the secret society of his family two weeks after I grazed my knee. He gave me that exact code to use when I needed help. It is the very reason I made it our SOS after we were ambushed by Dimitri in the parking lot of the warehouse. We needed a way to communicate that it was time for the other to run. I only agreed to his suggestion because I thought we were safe. I assumed since we were sheltered under Dimitri's umbrella, no one could touch us.

How stupid was I?

My focus returns to Caidyn when the noise of a door being slammed shut sounds down the line a short second before an engine being revved overtakes it. "That hasn't been Maddox's code for years, Demi. He gave it to you in middle school." I clamp a hand over my mouth when he says, "Then a couple of months ago, he made Landon, Saint, and I swear if we ever heard him say it, we would immediately get you out of Hopeton."

"No," I push out with a sob, aware of where he's going with this but incapable of believing what he is saying. "I only agreed to run if he was taken down." When I choke, Caidyn chokes. "You know that isn't the case. We'd know if that had happened."

"It was his life for Justine's, Demi. He had to pick." His horn honks when he slams his fist into the steering wheel of the car he's commanding. "Justine is barely hanging on, and that's physical. I have no fucking clue what's going on in that head of hers. She's strong, but fuck... this type of shit isn't real. Who orders for someone to be mauled by a dog?"

Oh god. This is worse than I realized.

"She's a human being, for fuck's sake. She is barely an adult—"

I cut his ramblings short by muttering, "It's my fault."

"What?" Caidyn asks. "How could this be your fault?"

I swallow down the bile scorching my throat before answering, "Max attacked Col. He gnawed on his arm." I feel the blood methodologically draining from my veins. "Justine's punishment was meant for me. She was attacked because of me." I'm exhausted, drained of the will to live, and slightly hormonal, but not even the naïveté of a child could hide the truth for a second longer. "And the same thing will happen to Maddox if I don't intervene." As I snatch up my keys from the desk and Max's leash, I say, "This is how my uncle operates. If he can't get what he wants, he goes after the people associated with them... Justine, Maddox, then you. He'll continue going down the list until he either grows bored or he gets what he wants. *I'm* who he wants, Caidyn." I bang my heaving chest with my fist. "*Me.* And I'm going to give him who he wants because nothing he could do to me would hurt more than losing Maddox."

"Dem—"

After dragging my phone away from my ear, I hit the end button on the screen, foiling Caidyn's plan to talk me out of my scheme, then I bob down in front of Max. "I'm sorry, buddy. I know you think this is your fight, but it isn't. I can't risk him hurting you too because he's angry at me, so you need to stay here." I click his lead onto his collar before banding my arms around his fat yet adorable head. "If you can get over your neurosis of men, Chef Jude knows how to cook. You'll be in heaven if you give him the chance to prove himself."

I smile when Max stands on all fours while licking his lips. He truly is the smartest dog in the world. So much so, he whimpers like I'm breaking his heart when I lift one side of my cousin's ginormous desk to slip the handle of his leash under one leg. Since I can lift the desk, I'm certain Max will have no issues dragging it across the room when I leave without him, but the desk is too wide to fit through the door. He'll be trapped in here until the morning shift at Petretti's starts.

"Be a good boy, Max. It's better to be bad sometimes than all the time." *I'm about to learn that the hard way.*

I scrub behind his pointed ears one final time before I race toward my future. If the rumblings in the sky are anything to go by, it will be as bleak and depressing as the howls Max releases when I slip into the driver's seat of Caidyn's jeep without him hot on my tail.

MADDOX

My shirt is soaked in blood. I'm nicked and bruised from the Rottweiler's obvious annoyance about me ending his bout before he claimed the ultimate trophy—my sister's life—and my heart is damaged beyond repair, but not one of those things are associated with the three goons sitting across from me, waiting with bated breath for Col to give them the go-ahead.

I had no intention of following the pledge I made when Col tossed Demi into our negotiation as if she is a bargaining chip. I merely said anything he wanted to hear, aware years of training award me the endurance to suffer hours of torture. By the time Col realized Demi was hiding in plain sight, my brothers would have found the message I wrote for Demi on the phone I stuffed into the pocket of Justine's dress after checking her for a pulse. Demi would be far from Hopeton, Justine would be getting the medical attention she needed, and I'd be able to die in peace knowing they were both safe.

When I was shoved into the middle SUV in a line of many, it appeared as if everything was going to plan. I spotted the taillights of Rocco's Buick race away from the Petretti compound, Col's men made a show out of cracking their knuckles during our twenty-minute drive to a residence hidden in the hills miles out of Hopeton, and I was shackled to a chair in the basement of a mansion-like property hours ago.

I am a sitting fucking duck, yet not one punch has been thrown.

I'm truly lost on Col's gameplan. He's ruthless, sordid, and doesn't have a moral bone in his body, so he can't be overly smart. Bullies use violence because they can't use intelligence. I was certain my ruse would be implemented without a hiccup. Now I have no fucking clue which way is up.

My eyes lift from my blood-soaked hands when the burn of pure evil scalds my head. Col is staring straight at me. His grin is smug, but it has nothing on the fire that blazes through his eyes when the door I was dragged through hours ago pops open. I wait for the putrid scent of a dog's coat wet with my sister's blood to plume my senses. I'm left reeling when the scent isn't close to the one I am anticipating. It's floral and feminine, a smell I'd recognize no matter how dire the circumstances.

"No!"

Demi isn't meant to be here.

She should have been hundreds of miles out of Hopeton by now.

I'm forced back into my seat by the brutal zap of a taser. The electrical current bolting throughout my body stiffens my muscles in an instant, but nothing can stop my eyes from trekking Demi's solemn walk across the room. Her hair is down and flowing around her shoulders, the clothes she was wearing when she stood across from me in the cabin have been replaced with a floral dress, and her face is wearing an expression I've never seen it wear before. She's here, but she isn't. So close, yet so far away. She's a shell of the woman who stood across from me demanding fairer judgment only months ago.

Just as Demi kneels in front of her uncle, the zap making my nervous system shut down momentarily suspends. I try to move. I try to get to Demi before Col can run his hand down her head like Demi does to Max any time he behaves, but my legs refuse to cooperate. They're heavy like lead and throbbing as much as the vein in Demi's neck when her uncle dips his chin to whatever she is whispering in his ear.

They chat for barely half a minute before Col helps Demi to her feet. He parades his niece in front of me, holding her hand high in the air like he's introducing a regal princess to her servants.

His ruse would be more effective if Demi didn't shatter the fairy tale by mouthing six little words that break my heart into a million pieces, *"It's just one of those days."*

When I freeze, muted by shock, Col guides Demi to a door opposite from the one she entered only moments ago. A strength unlike anything I've ever experienced surges through me when someone inside the room switches on the lights. It's a similar size structure as the one Justine was mauled in, except it doesn't have a vicious, fang-drooling animal waiting to savage Demi. There is a king-size bed and a wall filled with bondage paraphernalia.

When my roar snaps the rope circling my ankles, the man

who tased me back into my seat attempts to do it for the second time. I foil his endeavor by spinning around so fast, the stainless-steel chair I'm bound to knocks the taser out of his hand and sends him stumbling backward. A warrior cry parts my lips when I break his nose with my boot. He's so shocked by my unexpected violence, he doesn't attempt to protect his face when I ram my boot into it. I stomp and stomp and stomp until his face caves in and a third man joins us.

With my hands useless, I use my head to subdue him instead of my fists. I headbutt him like my brain isn't throbbing against my skull, then crack his sternum with a quick front projected kick. He isn't dead like the man with a now unrecognizable face, but he's down for the count, windless and unsure as to what the fuck just happened.

I almost reach the room Demi is in when the chair I'm carrying around like a tortoise shell is yanked backward. The force of the blond man's jerk untethers the rope around my wrists. With a move I've only seen in staged WWE fights, I spin around, snatch up the chair toppling toward the floor, smash it over his head, then send him flying away from me with the same front-propelled kick that pacified his friend.

With the room in lockdown and reeking of death, I race for the mirrored wall of the room Demi was guided into. "Demi!"

Memories of the time I banged my bloody fist on the glass partition in the ER of Mercer Private smack into me when I do the same to the two-way mirror separating Demi from me. The door Col forced her through is deadbolted with multiple locks, so I have no choice but to smash through the glass. It could be bulletproof, but that doesn't mean shit when you have a man enraged enough to slaughter a hundred men without remorse.

"Dem—"

My second shout of her name is cut short by the mirror effect of the wall fading away to glass. Demi is standing directly in front of me. Her dress has been removed, tears are careening down her cheeks, and she has a gun butted against her temple.

"Look at me," I demand when her drenched eyes stray away from mine for the quickest second to take in the carnage behind me. I did what needed to be done to save her, but that doesn't mean I'm proud of the maniac I've become. "Just keep looking at me, okay? It's going to be all right. I'm right fucking here. I'm not going anywhere."

When Demi's eyes return to mine, Col demands her to her knees. A squeak pops from her lips when she doesn't jump to his command quickly enough. He forces her to kneel in front of him by pulling roughly on her hair.

I smash my fists into the glass enough to make it wobble when Col uses a knife to remove Demi's bra and panties. They slide off her shuddering body like ice cream left outside on a hot summer's day.

"No!" I scream with a mangled roar when Col drags the tip of his blade up the galley between Demi's breasts. His pressure isn't enough to kill her, but it is deep enough to leave a scar. "Look at me, baby. Keep your eyes on me," I beg when Demi drops her gaze to the stream of blood rolling down her midsection.

She's quick to acknowledge the command in my tone, proving she is lucid, but I know she's hurting. There's so much pain in her big blue eyes, so much hurt. She's as devastated as me and very much confused.

"I love you," she mouths to me when Col moves his blade from her collarbone to her neck.

"I love you back," I say out loud, unashamed by the wetness in my eyes or the love I developed for her in a short period of time. I love this woman enough to kill without remorse. I can't express how much she means to me better than that.

When the tip of Col's blade digs into the vein thrumming in Demi's neck, air catches in my throat. He's going to kill his own blood to teach me a lesson, to prove how far he's willing to go to remain the king of his realm, and there isn't a fucking thing I can do about it.

Desperate, I snatch up the stainless-steel chair dumped in the middle of the death-scented space before tossing it into the glass separating me from the woman I love. It bounces off the seemingly impenetrable glass and nicks my face on the way by, but it doesn't end my campaign. I slam my fists into the splinter it caused to the bulletproof material, aware nothing will hurt more than seeing Demi killed directly in front of me.

While roaring like a wounded animal, I punch and punch and punch until the glass cracks, and a taser brings me to my knees. Even with her uncle holding her head back by a brutal clutch of her hair, Demi stares straight at me, her strength unwavering even moments from death.

It is proven without a doubt when she braces one of her tiny hands on the glass separating us and breathes, "It's just one of those days," before Col slices his knife to the left, silencing us both.

To be continued in Ox, available now!

Facebook: facebook.com/authorshandi

Instagram: instagram.com/authorshandi

Email: authorshandi@gmail.com

Reader's Group: bit.ly/ShandiBookBabes

Website: authorshandi.com

Newsletter: http://eepurl.com/cyEzNv

If you enjoyed this book, please leave a review.

ACKNOWLEDGMENTS

The page where I never know what to write. The past couple of weeks have been difficult for my family. My husband's dad is dying, my mum finished her last round of chemo, and although my dad keeps quiet on his health battles, he had a triple bypass only two years ago that is still giving him hell.

It's been a tiresome couple of weeks, but we are starting to see the light at the end of the tunnel. Chris has spent more time with his dad the past three weeks than he has the past seven years. My mother's health is improving, and my dad looks set to retire in a couple of months.

This book took longer for me to write, but that more had to do with the fact there was still so much story to tell. I'm glad I decided to make it a trilogy otherwise you'd still be waiting for this instalment.

As I write this, I am up to the final chapter in Ox, Maddox's final book. Then I have the epilogue to go. It has been a long process that's drained me, but I have loved learning Maddox's story.

I hope you have too.

Until next time.

Shandi xx

ALSO BY SHANDI BOYES

Denotes Standalone Books

<u>Perception Series</u>

<u>Saving Noah</u> *

<u>Fighting Jacob</u> *

<u>Taming Nick</u> *

<u>Redeeming Slater</u> *

<u>Saving Emily</u>

<u>Wrapped Up with Rise Up</u>

<u>Protecting Nicole</u> *

<u>Enigma</u>

<u>Enigma</u>

<u>Unraveling an Enigma</u>

<u>Enigma The Mystery Unmasked</u>

<u>Enigma: The Final Chapter</u>

<u>Beneath The Secrets</u>

<u>Beneath The Sheets</u>

<u>Spy Thy Neighbor</u> *

<u>The Opposite Effect</u> *

<u>I Married a Mob Boss</u> *

Second Shot *

The Way We Are

The Way We Were

Sugar and Spice *

Lady In Waiting

Man in Queue

Couple on Hold

Enigma: The Wedding

Silent Vigilante

Hushed Guardian

Quiet Protector

Enigma: An Isaac Retelling

Twisted Lies *

Bound Series

Chains

Links

Bound

Restrain

The Misfits *

Nanny Dispute *

Russian Mob Chronicles

Nikolai: A Mafia Prince Romance

Nikolai: Taking Back What's Mine

Nikolai: What's Left of Me

Nikolai: Mine to Protect

Asher: My Russian Revenge *

Nikolai: Through the Devil's Eyes

Trey *

The Italian Cartel

Dimitri

Roxanne

Reign

Mafia Ties (Novella)

Maddox

Demi

Ox

Rocco *

Clover *

Smith *

RomCom Standalones

Just Playin' *

Ain't Happenin' *

The Drop Zone *

Very Unlikely *

False Start *

<u>**Short Stories - Newsletter Downloads**</u>

Christmas Trio *

Falling For A Stranger *

<u>**One Night Only Series**</u>

Hotshot Boss *

Hotshot Neighbor *

<u>**The Bobrov Bratva Series**</u>

Wicked Intentions *

Sinful Intentions *

Devious Intentions *

Deadly Intentions *